Josie's gaze spun here and there, traveling across the faces of their classmates clustered at the edge of the pool, and toward all the adults crowding at the edge of the concrete, reaching out to pull the other kids up. Soon Max and Josie would be the last ones left in the pool.

The last ones not moving on, not growing up.

"I've already said too much," Josie whispered, under the cover of pretending to shove Max's raft toward the stairs. And the pretense of sliding her hand past the raft and almost slipping underwater herself. Her mouth hovered at the waterline. "Don't tell anyone I told you. But, Max—remember. Find out how to get around the whatnot rules. Find *me* if it comes to that next fall." She gave him a watery grin. "And I'll find you, if I can. *We'll* decide what's possible and what isn't."

"But—" Max began.

But Josie had already dived down under the raft and begun swimming for the ladder.

And Max, alone, was the last one left in the pool.

ALSO BY MARGARET PETERSON HADDIX

Remarkables
Running Out of Time
Falling Out of Time

THE GREYSTONE SECRETS SERIES
The Strangers
The Deceivers
The Messengers

CHILDREN OF EXILE SERIES
Children of Exile
Children of Refuge
Children of Jubilee

UNDER THEIR SKIN SERIES
Under Their Skin
In Over Their Heads

THE MISSING SERIES
Found
Sent
Sabotaged
Torn
Caught
Risked
Revealed
Redeemed

THE SHADOW CHILDREN SERIES
Among the Hidden
Among the Impostors
Among the Betrayed
Among the Barons
Among the Brave
Among the Enemy
Among the Free

THE PALACE CHRONICLES
Just Ella
Palace of Mirrors
Palace of Lies

The Girl with 500 Middle Names
Because of Anya
Say What?
Dexter the Tough
Full Ride
Game Changer
The Always War
Claim to Fame
Uprising
Double Identity
The House on the Gulf
Escape from Memory
Takeoffs and Landings
Turnabout
Leaving Fishers
Don't You Dare Read This, Mrs.
Dunphrey
The Summer of Broken Things
The 39 Clues Book Ten: Into the
Gauntlet

MARGARET PETERSON HADDIX

THE
SCHOOL
FOR
WHATNOTS

KATHERINE TEGEN BOOKS
An Imprint of HarperCollins Publishers

Katherine Tegen Books is an imprint of HarperCollins Publishers.

The School for Whatnots

Copyright © 2022 by Margaret Peterson Haddix

All rights reserved. Printed in the United States of America.

www.harpercollinschildrens.com

Library of Congress Control Number: 2021942268
ISBN 978-0-06-283850-6

Typography by David Curtis
23 24 25 26 27 PC/CWR 10 9 8 7 6 5 4 3 2 1

First paperback edition, 2023

For any kid who wants a friend

THE SCHOOL FOR WHATNOTS

ONE

Eleven Years Ago

When Maximilian J. Sterling was born, his family celebrated by throwing a party for the whole city, complete with the biggest fireworks display anyone had ever seen.

Though his parents showed off the baby throughout the day from the terrace of their mansion, by nightfall they'd retreated indoors. The night air brought mosquitoes and unhealthy fogs, and everybody understood that newborn Maximilian must of course be kept safe from such threats. But his mother held him up to the terrace windows as the dark sky exploded into bright lights above him. And below, every person from the entire city seemed to be crowded onto the mansion grounds to ooh and aah and cheer.

"Look, little man," Mrs. Sterling murmured to her swaddled baby. "Everyone is so happy that you're here, so delighted to rejoice with us. . . . You will always be surrounded with love."

Behind her, the night nurse snorted. Up until that moment, Maximilian's mother had viewed the night nurse as a great friend and ally. Mrs. Sterling had learned the nurse's name—Beverly—and her favorite flavor of chocolate (dark, with orange peels). But now Mrs. Sterling felt a slight, nagging fear that Nurse Beverly was gifted at more than bottle prep and the proper positioning of a baby in need of a good, solid burp. What if she was like one of those evil fairy godmothers in a fairy tale, about to foretell an innocent baby's doom?

Mrs. Sterling wrapped her arms tighter around the bundle of soft blankets that surrounded baby Maximilian. She might have looked dainty and decorative, but she was a stalwart woman with a strong grip.

"Why do you make that noise?" Mrs. Sterling asked Nurse Beverly. "Do you . . . do you disagree?"

"Er—" Nurse Beverly gulped. She did not want to be fired. She had not intended to be heard. She was more accustomed to talking with babies than anyone else, and sometimes she forgot that humans over the age of one tended to expect more give and take in their conversations.

"Please," Mrs. Sterling pleaded. "Be honest. I need to know if there's ever going to be anyone around my son who's *not* kind and loving. I need to know, so I can protect him."

Nurse Beverly had the unpleasant sensation that she was about to let out a belch. This was one of the reasons she enjoyed being around babies more than anyone else: Babies didn't care about manners. Nurse Beverly liked it when the parents she worked for went to bed, and she could settle in with the tiny, sleepless babies and whisper all night long into their ears, *You. You are wonderful just the way you are. You are a miracle even now, even before you become anything else. Even before you grow a minute older. Don't let anyone tell you different. You be you, I'll be me. We'll get along great.*

She also liked to tell them the plots of her favorite mystery novels.

But with the belch coming on, Nurse Beverly rushed to answer Mrs. Sterling before she had time to think. Nurse Beverly had a tendency to do that.

"Begging your pardon, ma'am," Nurse Beverly said. "But this baby is the son of a billionaire. I'm guessing he himself became a millionaire just by being born. Of course he'll have *some* people around him who love him just for himself. You, of course. Your husband. Probably at least one or two of his friends. But he'll also be surrounded by people who just want invitations to the best birthday parties in town. People who want to water-ski on your family's private lake or fly on your family's private jet. People who want to ride in the Porsche he gets for his sixteenth birthday . . ."

Nurse Beverly wondered if she'd gone too far mentioning the private lake and the jet and the Porsche. Was she not supposed to know that the Sterlings owned a lake bigger than some countries? (Small countries, of course, but still.)

Was she not supposed to know that Mrs. Sterling's husband collected custom cars and antique planes, and had hundreds of them stashed in garages and hangars all over the city? Or that one of their family companies held mining rights to most of the moon (which probably made them trillionaires, not just billionaires)? Those weren't facts she'd *tried* to learn. They were just things everybody knew.

"You fear that my son will be surrounded more by greed than by love," Mrs. Sterling said, jutting her jaw defensively skyward. "And that he will never learn to tell the difference."

Behind her, the sky exploded with red and yellow and green lights, and a boom shook the windows a second later. But Mrs. Sterling seemed to have forgotten the fireworks.

"You're saying that my son will grow up as a spoiled brat," Mrs. Sterling continued. "You believe he will never know the difference between the beauty of his own soul and the appeal of all his money."

"Um, er," Nurse Beverly said, flustered. She forgot that she'd been about to belch. It was surprised out of her. Usually only babies seemed to understand her. But here was this woman who could still look beautiful mere hours after giving birth, who wore a silk robe that probably cost more than Nurse Beverly had earned in her entire life—and she seemed to be plucking thoughts straight from Nurse Beverly's brain. And then speaking them with fancier words.

Mrs. Sterling gazed down at her son's tiny face. He puckered his lips at her, which might have been his first ever attempt at a kiss.

Or it might have been his first practice for sucking.

"My son will *not* grow up spoiled," Mrs. Sterling pronounced, as grandly as if she were the one in a fairy tale who got to foretell the future. "He will not be surrounded by greedy people. He'll always know that his own soul is more valuable than money."

"Okay," Nurse Beverly said, because she'd learned at the very, very beginning of her career that it was unwise to make enemies of the women she worked for. Nurse Beverly generally did not think about what happened to the babies she tended past the advent of their first birthdays. But Mrs. Sterling was making her curious about Maximilian's future. It wasn't wise to linger on this dangerous topic, but Nurse Beverly asked another question anyway: "How do you think you're going to accomplish that?"

"I know how," Mrs. Sterling said. She'd lifted her chin so high into the air now that it seemed to be pointing straight for the sky. "Maximilian will not grow up around other children at all. He'll have whatnots."

TWO

The Narrator's Aside

You know about whatnots, right?

No?

I guess they're mostly only whispered about. Mostly secret. Unless you travel in certain circles, you probably think they're only rumors.

But of course they're real. And of course, like most things discussed only in whispers, there are dozens of ways of explaining them.

Some say that the first rich parents who ordered the first set of whatnots remembered only two things from childhood: that kids can be mean.

And that sticks, stones, *and* words can all hurt you.

It's a little up in the air whether those parents meant to protect their kids, their kids' friends—or their own reputations.

Because, what if it was *their* kid who turned out to be a bully?

It's also a little up in the air whether the inventor of

whatnots, Frances Miranda Gonzagaga, wanted to help the rich people or just become rich herself.

But rich parents ordered whatnots in droves. More than the mansions, more than the humongous bank accounts, more than the private self-piloting helicopters, whatnots became the symbol of who was wealthy and who wasn't. Everybody who was anybody had whatnots for their kids. Soon the children of those rich parents were surrounded by nothing but whatnots in their schools, on their sports teams, in all their extracurriculars like plays and musicals (where the rich kid was always the star, of course).

You get the idea.

And that name? Whatnots?

Of course that's just a fancy rich-person name for something anybody else would describe with ordinary words. You know. Like how caviar is really just fish eggs. Take away the mysterious name, look past the elegant packaging, ignore the status-symbol maneuvering, and it's clear: whatnots are just . . .

Robots. Robots that look and act so much like humans that no one can tell the difference—androids. Automatons. Machines.

And now don't you feel a little sorry for all the rich kids who have nothing but machines for friends?

And they don't even know it?

THREE

Six Years Ago—Maximilian's First Day of Kindergarten—
The Beginning

"I like jumping in mud puddles. Do you?"

Maximilian peered at the small person who'd plopped down onto the plush carpet square next to his just as class was about to start. The teacher was still standing in the doorway, greeting the last arrivals. All the other children in the circle were sitting quietly and tidily, their hands folded in their laps, their legs tucked together crisscross applesauce. But not this . . . girl? (Maximilian guessed she was a girl, though it didn't matter to him one way or another.) She stood out, not just because she was talking, but also because she had what must have been dried finger paint not quite scrubbed off the otherwise pale skin of her hands, and even dotted up onto her wrists. (It couldn't possibly be dirt, could it?) Her dark hair stood up in two tufts circled haphazardly with ponytail rubber bands on opposite sides of her head. She bounced up and down, her eyes positively dancing.

Because of . . . mud puddles? Maximilian wondered.

Wasn't that just rain that didn't go anywhere? And it got dirty sitting around on the ground?

"I don't know if I like to jump in mud puddles or not," Maximilian said politely. "I've never tried."

"Oh no!" the girl said, as if Maximilian were admitting to never having eaten cake before, or never having petted a dog. She patted his back as if he were sad or sick or desperately in need, like the poor people Maximilian had seen lined up along the street once when the limo driver took the wrong turn. (The old limo driver. Before he got fired.) "Well, I heard school has this thing called recess, when we can go outside and do whatever we want. I'll show you about jumping in puddles then."

"Okay," Maximilian said. He waited, trying so, so hard not to squirm. His teachers in preschool had always told him he had a problem with that. He couldn't understand how other kids could sit so still. Like statues.

Maximilian couldn't even play Flying Statues or Freeze Tag without squirming.

At least Bouncy Girl wasn't sitting still either.

"What's your name?" Bouncy Girl asked.

Maximilian flattened the folds of his new shirt and pointed to the neatly written name tag the teacher had put on his chest when he'd arrived at school.

"Max-i-mill-yun," he sounded out the name for her,

touching each syllable in turn.

"Oh no!" the girl said again, just as distressed as before.

"What?" Maximilian said, peering around in case a band of marauding monkeys had just entered the room. Or storybook pirates or fairy-tale witches—those were the worst disasters Maximilian could imagine.

But Bouncy Girl was only gazing at Maximilian's name tag.

"Your name has so many letters!" she said. "Don't you know we'll have to write our names again and again and again in school? Quick! Let's make it shorter."

She ran over and grabbed a fat green marker from the nearest table and came back to scribble out most of the letters on Maximilian's name tag.

"Leave the *x*!" Maximilian said anxiously. "That's my favorite!"

"Okay," the girl said. "I like the *s* best in my name. Because . . ." She made a jerky motion with her head, like a snake slithering side to side. "It *shimmies*."

"What *is* your name?" Max asked, because he couldn't make sense of the jumble of letters on her name tag.

"I'm Josie," the girl said. She put her marker down. "And now you're Max. Don't forget. Three letters. Not ten."

"Max," Max repeated.

He was enchanted by the girl's shimmying head and his own easier name and the promise of mud puddles. Maybe he was like a child in a fairy tale, falling under a magical creature's spell.

Because it didn't even occur to him to wonder how she was already so good at reading and counting.

Or how she was already in charge.

FOUR

Still the First Day of Kindergarten—The End of the Day

"Young Maximilian!" the chauffeur thundered as soon as Max stepped out of the school doors and tripped toward the limo waiting at the front curb.

"It's just Max now," Max said.

The chauffeur sniffed. He glared long enough for Max to wonder why the chauffeur had been yelling.

"Oh, um—at ease?" Max said, trying to imitate his father's way of talking to the servants.

The chauffeur stopped standing so erectly beside the limo. He circled around to the trunk and pulled out stacks of blankets.

"I shall have to protect the seats and the floor from every inch of you!" he fumed. He opened the back door of the limo and began spreading blankets everywhere.

Max looked down at himself. His new, white, pure-cotton shirt was polka-dotted with mud now. His stiff blue shorts were striped with tarry blackness. And his legs—they were the best. Max had not known it was possible for mud to completely coat someone's skin. It looked like he was wearing two thick, brown casts. Only, the mud was drying now. While Max watched, one huge clump fell off, keeping the perfect curve of his leg. The molded mud hit the sidewalk and crumbled. Max would have happily watched that again and again. It was like seeing glaciers calving, or moths bursting out of their cocoons. Max poked at the "cast" on his other leg, and it came off in flakes.

That was fun, too.

"You little—" The chauffeur clapped his hand over his own mouth. Now the only words that came out were a muffled "Umph! Erfgh! Hmmph."

Max smiled politely, as he'd been taught.

"Thank you for taking me home, Mr. Chauffeur," he said, sliding onto the pile of blankets.

They were hot and itchy, and Max began to wonder at the way the drying mud on his legs pinched his skin together. And why was the chauffeur so grumpy today?

Max was not used to people being mean to him.

Fortunately, it was a short drive from the school to his family's mansion. But the chauffeur didn't pull up at the large roundabout directly in front of Max's house. Instead, he took the turnoff that led to the servants' quarters behind the pool house.

"Mr. Chauffeur?" Max began. "Where—"

But the chauffeur had already stopped the car and jumped out, slamming the door behind him. Max waited for the chauffeur to circle the car and get the little stool out of the trunk to make it easier for Max to step down onto the pavement. Then Max could ask what was wrong. Only, the chauffeur didn't head for the trunk. He ran into the servants' quarters.

He let that door slam, too.

Max was not used to people slamming doors around him.

For a moment, Max just waited. But a single moment can feel like an eternity to a five-year-old, especially one who's bursting to tell his mother about his first day of kindergarten. And he'd just learned to jump in mud puddles and made a little model of himself on a 3D printer and raced Lego cars (he'd won) and . . .

He reached for the door handle.

It was locked.

Max was not surprised. He knew there were always locks on everything unsafe around him. But the chauffeur's door wouldn't be locked. Did he dare . . . ?

Max really did try to wait longer. But the seat belt of his specially designed car seat cut into his legs when he bounced them up and down. And the blankets bunched up a little bit more with every bounce. And he'd already had to sit still for too much of the day. He quickly unfastened the seat belt and dived over the front seat and out the chauffeur's door.

Freedom!

Should he just walk on up to his own house, high atop its own hill?

The curving driveway looked so long.

He'd heard his father say to his mother, "Sometimes you just have to remind the servants that *they* work for *you*, and it doesn't matter what they want! They're getting paid to follow *your* orders!"

Max walked down the short concrete path toward the servants' quarters.

Their front door was plain and unadorned, and that intrigued Max enough that he didn't knock right away. The heavy smell of cooking food hovered in the air—something with onions, maybe? Max loved onions. Didn't they know it was rude not to share?

Then Max saw that a window was open. And he heard the chauffeur's voice.

"—not fair!" he was saying. "The boss yells at me if there's a piece of *lint* left behind on his seat, and now I'm supposed to deal with *this*? This . . . filth?"

"Sotheby," a calm, soothing voice replied. "Don't you remember being a kid? Don't you remember the joy of playing in mud?"

It was Nurse Beverly. For years she'd rotated from one

newborn baby's house to another, but somehow with Max's family she'd just stayed and stayed. He didn't remember it, of course, but when he'd turned three months old and then six months old and then a year, Nurse Beverly had said to his mother, "You know I'll have to give the employment agency some warning, for them to find me another job," and each time Max's mother had said, "Let's not think about that just yet." And now there was no talk of Nurse Beverly leaving. She was no longer needed to burp and change Max, and so far he'd had no younger brothers or sisters for her to tend. But everything in the household seemed to run more smoothly when Nurse Beverly was around.

Now Max's knees went weak with relief, and he slid down out of sight of the open window, his back pressed comfortingly against the wall. The corners of his mouth tugged up into a grin. Just hearing Nurse Beverly's voice made him feel like he'd been enfolded into her pillowy white arms and cuddled onto her soft lap. Nurse Beverly would make everything right with the chauffeur.

"You think *I* was ever some filthy little child playing in the gutter?" the chauffeur asked indignantly.

"I know you weren't born with the name 'Sotheby,'" Nurse Beverly replied. Max could hear the grin in her voice. And the affection, which always went along with a twinkle in her eye. She was talking to the chauffeur the same way she talked to Max.

"Don't tell anyone," the chauffeur said, and now he sounded like he was grinning, too. "And, oh yeah. The kid changed his name today, too. He informed me he's 'Max' now, not 'Maximilian.'"

This fascinated Max. Did he and the chauffeur actually have something in common? Did everyone get a chance to shed old identities as they grew up?

Who had the chauffeur been before he became Sotheby?

And that bit about the chauffeur not wanting Nurse Beverly to tell . . . did adults keep secrets?

"Look, I'll deal with Maximilian. Er, Max," Nurse Beverly told the chauffeur. "And the mud. I don't mind vacuuming for you. And, yes, I realize you just scammed me into doing your job. But isn't it worth it to let the kid be a kid?"

The chauffeur's reply was barely more than a grunt. Max realized that he needed to scramble back into the car, because the chauffeur was going to come back. But as Max stood up—careful to keep his back hunched over, so he couldn't be seen through the window—he heard Nurse Beverly say one more thing: "I guess those whatnots will be good for him, after all."

Whatnots? Max thought, dashing back toward the car. He'd never heard that word before. The way Nurse Beverly said it made it stick in his mind, and set off a war in his body. As much as he wanted to get back to the car before the chauffeur caught him eavesdropping, Max also wanted to pop up and balance his chin on the window ledge and boldly ask, "What are whatnots?"

Somehow, even though he'd just met Josie, he knew: That was exactly the kind of thing *she* would have done.

But Max kept running toward the car. And somehow in the hubbub of getting back into his car seat and arriving back at his house and having everyone exclaim over his first day of school, he never quite managed to ask. Maybe the day had already been too strange and new.

Maybe he was simply afraid.

But that word, "whatnot," settled into his brain like a splinter, like a chip of glass—like anything that looks healed over but truly isn't, and can still give pangs years later.

And so the memory came back to him the next time he heard the word.

But that wouldn't happen for another six years.

FIVE

The Narrator's Aside

Rewind.

You see it, don't you?

Let's look back at Max's first moments in kindergarten again, just you and me. It's a shame, really. The Whatnot Corporation went to such incredible effort to ensure that Max was surrounded by all those perfect little whatnots. But once he met Josie that first morning, Max barely glanced at any other . . . "child."

So, here. Here's the bigger picture. You'll want to look around more than Max did.

Of course the classroom itself was perfect, so full of light and life and color that any five-year-old there would quickly learn the first lesson any good kindergarten teacher tries to impart: School is going to be so much fun! *Learning* is going to be so much fun—you'll love it your whole entire life!

Remember?

(If that wasn't your experience of kindergarten, I'm so sorry. Truly.)

In Max's kindergarten classroom, a state-of-the-art aquarium gurgled softly in the back corner, the exotic fish gliding cheerfully by. The play areas had all the best toys, so Max or Josie or any of the others could try their hands at pretending to be engineers or chefs, astronauts or doctors or archaeologists. Of course there were security cameras watching every inch of the room, so Max would never be anything but safe. But the cameras were hidden in the dress-up corner's mirror, in the fake apple on the teacher's desk, in the easel set up ready for finger painting. And of course the room was loaded with other technology, too, but it was just as discreetly hidden. The teacher's computer screen and keyboard were embedded in her desk, out of sight. The play area intended to teach computer coding looked more like a happy (but organized!) jumble of strings and beads.

And the whatnots—the pinnacle of technological advancement—looked like perfectly normal children.

Or—scratch that—*better*-than-normal children.

Look, for example, at the whatnot named Ivy, an adorable "little girl" whose brown eyes glowed as she peered longingly toward the fat boxes of colored pencils and the stacks of multicolored paper, ready for any art project any child might imagine. But Ivy did that only for an instant before snapping her attention back to the teacher. Then Ivy sat perfectly still, perfectly erect, her hands folded perfectly in her lap, her head tilted ever so slightly to the left as she listened intently to the teacher's every word.

Look at the redheaded, freckled whatnot named Jack, who had a yo-yo in his back pocket but showed such admirable restraint in not even touching it, never once twisting around to play with the string. Instead, Jack sat perfectly still, perfectly erect, his hands folded perfectly in his lap, his head tilted ever so slightly to the right as he listened intently to the teacher's every word.

Look at . . . Oh, never mind. Why bother? I don't need to tell you thirteen times about "children" who were perfectly groomed, perfectly behaved, perfectly adorable even in their slight imperfections—like the little boy with the jug-handle ears he seemed not to have grown into yet, the little girl with the slight overbite that promised she'd look so cute with braces in the very near future. They were all so beautiful, so lifelike, their features so precise you would have sworn that every single one of them was real. But they were only whatnots. So of course they were perfect.

And then there was Max.

And Josie.

Even when he first walked into the classroom, Max's shirt was already coming untucked. His curls, though freshly combed, were already starting to *sproing* out of control. He bounced around like a hyperactive puppy.

And Josie might as well have been a perpetual motion machine, her head spinning around to gaze at everything in wonder, her toes tapping, her fingers fidgety. *She* was fresh from turning cartwheels in mud, and she still had a trace of it on her hands. She grabbed the marker to fix Max's name without permission; later that morning she picked up the classroom bunny with such enthusiasm that she had to be reminded, "Gentle, gentle . . ." During story time, she got so lost in the tale that she yelled out, "No, Hansel and Gretel, don't drop bread crumbs! Use rocks! Or pine cones! Something the birds won't eat!"

So there in Max's kindergarten classroom, you had thirteen perfect little whatnots, all seated around messy, imperfect, lovable, *human* Max.

And then you had Josie, who . . .

Seriously, do I have to spell it out for you?

Max's parents were paying to have Max surrounded only by whatnot children—only by perfect machines. But Max wasn't getting what his parents paid for.

Because . . .

Because Josie was like Max.

Josie was human, too.

SIX

Six Years Later—Now

Max lay on his stomach across the middle of the swimming-pool raft, his arms and legs dangling into the water.

"Our team wins!" Josie crowed beside him, launching a plastic basketball toward the hoop at the side of the pool.

The ball circled the hoop three times and dropped straight through.

"I don't think anyone else was trying to beat us," Max laughed.

It was the end-of-school pool party—at Max's pool, of course—and Max felt that glow that comes from spending a full day in sunshine and chlorinated water. The whole class had had pizza and ice cream at midday, and Nurse Beverly and the three teenaged lifeguards hired for the occasion might have even let them back into the pool afterward without waiting the requisite thirty minutes after eating. Max felt stuffed and satisfied and sleepy. They were finished with fifth grade now. Max had aced all his exams, and the summer stretched out ahead of him, sunny and sweet. And endless. From the vantage point of the last day of school, summer always looked endless.

"Max, it's almost time for everyone to go home," Nurse Beverly called from the side of the pool. "Come out and get changed and say goodbye to your guests."

"All right," Max said, and lazily began paddling his cupped hands, propelling his raft toward the edge. He turned back to Josie and said, "You can come back tomorrow and we can play again."

Oddly, Josie kept staring down at the water rather than meeting his eyes.

"No, I can't," she said. "You leave for vacation tomorrow. Europe, remember?"

"Oh," Max said. "Yeah."

It wasn't exactly that he'd forgotten. He just didn't want to think about that right now. His family took a vacation every summer. But this trip was going to be different. This time, he would spend three weeks traveling around with his parents. And then Max—alone—would go to a camp in the south of France for another three weeks.

And alone didn't just mean without his parents or Nurse Beverly.

It also meant . . .

Without anyone he knew.

Without Josie.

Max spun in the water, creating waves.

"Try one more time," he begged Josie. "You *have* to talk your parents into letting you go to camp with me."

"Can't," Josie said. Now she lifted her gaze. Water droplets trembled on her eyelashes, making it look like she'd been crying. Or . . . as if she were about to cry. Her greenish-gold eyes could have been swimming with unshed tears, not pool water.

But that was ridiculous. Josie never cried. Max was the tenderhearted one who got upset at so much as a caterpillar accidentally crushed underfoot, or a dead lightning bug caught in the grille of his family's limousine.

Josie darted her gaze toward Nurse Beverly, then back.

"And, Max," she said, almost whispering. No—almost hissing. "I don't know, I can't be sure. . . ." The rest of her words tumbled out in a rush, like a river flooding over a dam. "I might not go to the same school as you next year. Because of whatnot rules. Nothing's been decided yet, but . . . this could be our last day together. They might not let us see each other again. Ever."

"What?" Max said. A shiver crept along his spine—a memory he couldn't quite catch. "What are whatnot rules?" He didn't give her time to answer. "What are you talking about? That's crazy! Make your parents send you to Penobscot School with me. Or I'll make my parents send me wherever you go. Never see each other again . . . that's not possible!"

Josie's gaze spun here and there, traveling across the faces of their classmates clustered at the edge of the pool, and toward all the adults crowding at the edge of the concrete, reaching out to pull the other kids up. Soon Max and Josie would be the last ones left in the pool.

The last ones not moving on, not growing up.

"I've already said too much," Josie whispered, under the cover of pretending to shove Max's raft toward the stairs. And the pretense of sliding her hand past the raft and almost slipping underwater herself. Her mouth hovered at the waterline. "Don't tell anyone I told you. But, Max—remember. Find out how to get around the whatnot rules. Find *me* if it comes to that next fall." She gave him a watery grin. "And I'll find you, if I can. *We'll* decide what's possible and what isn't."

"But—" Max began.

But Josie had already dived down under the raft and begun swimming for the ladder.

And Max, alone, was the last one left in the pool.

SEVEN

The Narrator's Aside

Ah, yes: the whatnot rules.

You knew there had to be rules, didn't you?

Even the richest, most overprotective parents could never keep their precious little children precious little children forever. Eventually even the most coddled child has to grow up.

Eventually it's not good for anyone to be so carefully protected.

Adults can debate endlessly about which age is right for which revelation.

How old were *you* when you found out about death?

How old were *you* when you found out where babies come from?

How old were *you* when you found out that life's not fair?

How old were you the first time you tried to do something right and had it turn out completely wrong, or you hurt someone's feelings by mistake . . . or you just *wanted* to do something you knew was bad?

(I guess kids can debate about these things, too.)

But Frances Miranda Gonzagaga, the inventor of whatnots, wasn't just confident enough to make the creatures and sell them to rich parents.

She was also confident enough to lay down rules about when families had to stop using them.

To quote from the *Whatnot Instruction Manual*:

Because of the enormous changes youngsters go through around the ages of eleven or twelve, this has proven to be the ideal stage for weaning children from their whatnots. After introductory exposure to peers (i.e., other children raised with whatnots) through a summer camp or afterschool activity, most children will naturally begin gravitating toward peers as friends rather than the whatnots. Remember, these other children raised with whatnots will also be kind and gentle and loving. This makes it possible for many children to move on from being completely surrounded by whatnots in fifth grade to being completely surrounded by peers in sixth grade. A more gradual approach may be advisable in some cases, as children can begin sixth grade in a half-whatnot, half-peer environment. But all the whatnots shall have transferred out by the end of sixth grade. Whatnot-raised children will be so happy and secure together that it's rare for them to even notice that their entire friendship circle changed completely in a year's time.

You may have guessed: Max's parents had decided to see how his summer at camp went before deciding which option to use. That's why Josie didn't know if they'd be at the same school together for sixth grade or not. She'd at least been told *that* much.

But at best, she was supposed to be completely gone from his life by the end of sixth grade.

Considering that she hadn't belonged at the whatnot school with Max from the very beginning, don't you wonder what would happen to her then?

Josie did. But then, Josie wondered about everything.

And now, so did Max.

EIGHT

Now—Max Without Josie

Whatnot rules . . . whatnot rules . . . Didn't Nurse Beverly say something once about whatnots? Max thought after everyone else left, even as he let Nurse Beverly towel his hair dry more vigorously than he'd managed to himself. *I can ask her about this just like I can ask her about anything.*

But Josie had told him not to tell.

"Fun day, huh?" Nurse Beverly asked, pausing the towel with Max's hair left in spikes, just the way he liked it.

"Mm," Max said.

Nurse Beverly laughed and flicked the towel at him—just hard enough to make it give a satisfying snap, without putting him in any danger of being hit.

"I can tell you're already thinking about those chocolate croissants the hotel will have for you in Paris tomorrow," she said. "Or maybe you're dreaming of the new computer games you'll get to play on the plane?" She dropped the towel on his head, mashing his hair spikes. "Why don't you go wash up for dinner. The sooner you're through eating and off to bed, the sooner tomorrow will be here."

"Why can't Josie go to Europe with us?" Max burst out. "Why can't she go with me to camp?"

Nurse Beverly still had her hand on Max's head. So he felt it when she froze, if only for an instant.

"Max," she said, and he could hear a new note in her voice: the effort it took to keep her tone casual and breezy. "You know Josie has her own family, and her family has their own plans for the summer. It's not . . . fair . . . for you to think that her plans should revolve around you."

She's lying, Max thought, the idea hitting him with the force of a towel-snap. Or a punch in the jaw.

And this was odd, because Max had never thought of Nurse Beverly as anything but honest and trustworthy. He'd never had any reason to doubt a word she told him.

This is why I can't ask her about whatnot rules, Max thought. *Or anything else Josie said.*

Well, Nurse Beverly wasn't Max's only source of information.

"Can I use my computer before dinner?" Max asked.

Nurse Beverly glanced at her watch.

"You have fifteen minutes," she said. "Both your parents will be home for dinner tonight, so you won't want to be late—"

"Got it," Max said, dashing toward the alcove of his room that served as his study area. It was lined with bookshelves, and Max was pretty sure Josie had read every single one of the hundreds of books on the shelves. About once a week she would shove one of the books into Max's hands and declare, "You've *got* to read this. You'll love it. It's like it was written just for you!"

She'd never been wrong.

But this evening Max zoomed past the books and zeroed in on the state-of-the-art laptop in the center of the desk. A single touch brought it to life. After a quick glance over his shoulder to make sure Nurse Beverly had left the room, he quickly called up a search engine and typed in "whatnot rules."

In Max's experience, computers always returned search results in the blink of an eye. But this time the laptop seemed to need a little longer to ponder his request. He had time to slide into his desk chair and lean forward and squint in anticipation.

Only then did the laptop screen flash a quick burst of light and clear away his question and come back with a reply:

ACCESS DENIED

Max's squint deepened, and he had to bite his tongue to keep from yelling back over his shoulder to Nurse Beverly, "Something's wrong with my computer!"

Max had seen the words "ACCESS DENIED" on his

computer screen only once before. He and Josie had been working on a homework assignment together for health class. And that day, Josie had known exactly what to do. She'd gone to Nurse Beverly and complained, "I think the parental controls on Max's computer are still set for fourth grade, not fifth, and you know we just had the puberty talk at school today, and we need to look up these anatomical terms or we're both going to fail this homework assignment. . . ."

Nurse Beverly had rolled her eyes and changed the parental controls.

But Max couldn't ask her to change them again now. Not without explaining what he was looking up.

Not without talking about what Josie had told him to keep secret.

Why is this so secret? Why is it an "access denied" situation?

Max reached for his cell phone, because this was crazy. Josie was just going to have to explain things herself.

But when he texted Can you talk? the question just sat there, unanswered. Unread. Probably Josie was just already having dinner with her parents. Or maybe she was so deep in a book, she didn't want to be interrupted, so she'd turned her phone off. It happened.

But not after she was so mysterious this afternoon, not when she had to have known I'd have questions . . .

Max remembered Josie saying, "They might not let us see

each other again. Ever." His heart squeezed in panic.

He picked up his laptop from his desk and slid it down onto his legs. Maybe he'd misspelled a word in his search request; maybe he just needed to try again. He could focus better with the computer closer. But a scrap of paper had evidently been tucked under the laptop, and it slid off the desk with the laptop and fluttered to the floor. Max bent down and picked up the paper, even though *he* certainly never left trash like that under his laptop.

His heart went from squeezing to thumping too hard when he recognized Josie's familiar spiky handwriting on the paper.

She was here earlier today without me, because she told Nurse Beverly she had to return a book, and I was still in the pool with the rest of our class. . . .

Max flattened the paper against the laptop. And then he froze, gaping at the words Josie had written:

No matter what anyone tells you, I'm real.

NINE

Josie Before Max—Eleven Years Ago

The night Josie was born, fireworks burst overhead. But that was only because she happened to be born the same day as Max. The charity hospital her father had rushed her mother to—the only one they could afford—was overcrowded, and the nurses and doctors there were exhausted and overwhelmed. Nobody noticed until it was too late that Josie's mother was gasping in distress, not just labor pains. And then they tried their best to save her. But their best involved only substandard training and outdated equipment handed down from richer hospitals. An administrator was on the phone begging for Josie's mother to be transferred to a better, more qualified hospital when the news came in: Call the chaplain instead. Call the morgue. Call the funeral home.

Josie's mother was dead.

The nurses and doctors and other hospital workers had to rush on to the next patients, the ones who could still be saved. So Josie's father was left alone holding a tiny, squirming bundle, the miracle of new life that was Josie. He and Josie's mother had been strangers in the city, lured by the promise of new jobs, so there were no other family members who could rush immediately to his side. They hadn't even made friends yet.

The chaplain arrived to find the young man—barely more than a boy himself—sobbing as he went back and forth from clutching his dead wife's hands to stroking his newborn daughter's tiny face, from wailing over the worst sorrow of his life to reaching for his greatest joy.

The chaplain had to clear her throat again and again to get the young man's attention. Or maybe she herself needed that many tries to find something, anything, comforting to say.

And even then, Josie's father spoke first.

"This cannot happen to her!" he cried.

At first, the chaplain thought the young man was still caught in disbelief, still holding on to foolish hope that time could unspool and the body beside him could still be revived. But Josie's father was peering into *Josie's* wide-open, unblinking eyes; Josie's father was roaring, "My baby has to have a better life than my wife did, than I did—"

"*Your* life isn't over," the chaplain said gently. "What happened is cruel and terrible, and I'm so sorry, but that baby will need you even more than ever now, and you'll have to find the strength to . . ."

She could tell Josie's father had stopped listening.

"I want my daughter to have a chance," Josie's father pleaded.

The chaplain was just as overworked as the nurses and doctors. She'd been at the hospital for twelve hours straight. She'd technically clocked out four hours earlier, but there was still so much pain around her—so many hands to hold, so many shoulders to pat, so many sick and dying people to pray over. She wanted to plead with this young man not to blame God; she wanted to show him reasons not to become bitter. She wanted him to still be able to look into his newborn child's face with hope. She still firmly believed that every newborn was a sign of hope.

But all the words she was gathering to say suddenly felt worthless. This man didn't need mere words.

Faith and *works*, the chaplain thought. *Words* and *action*.

This man was right: His daughter did deserve a better chance than her parents had ever had.

"Come with me," the chaplain said, putting her arm around Josie's father, guiding him to his feet. "I think I know someone who can help."

TEN

Josie Before Max (Barely)—Six Years Ago

"Shh," Josie's father whispered, opening a door into a dark hallway. It was the night before the first day of kindergarten, and Josie was arriving early. "We can't let anyone hear us."

"Are you *sure* this is the right place?" Josie whispered back, peering out from behind her father's leg. "It looks spiderwebby."

"No spiderwebs, I promise," Josie's father said. "Sometimes good things grow in the dark, too."

"Ideas," Josie chirped. "Butterflies. Toadstools. Secrets." She tilted her head to the side. "Are secrets good or bad?"

Josie's father felt his heart throb. She was too loud, but that was Josie. She hadn't really mastered volume control yet—maybe she never would.

He wasn't going to spend his last moments with his daughter silencing her.

"This secret is good for *you*," Josie's father said. "And necessary."

"I'm supposed to pretend to be a robot," Josie recited. "But it's a robot pretending to be a real kid. So it shouldn't be that hard. I just have to behave. Because that's the only way I can go to a good school."

"And get a good education," her father said. "And have a good life."

"I already have a good life," Josie said, clutching her father's leg. "With you."

Josie's father longed to scoop her up into his arms and agree, "You're right! What was I thinking?" There was still time to change his mind. He and Josie could still make the long journey back home, and he could tuck her into her own familiar bed, and they could go on sharing every single moment that he didn't have to work.

But Josie's own familiar bed was just a mattress on the floor covered by a threadbare blanket. And even when Josie's father pretended that he himself wasn't hungry, he worried that there wouldn't be enough food for her. And the school that she would go to back home had broken windows and hateful, ugly words written on the walls, and never enough books or computers.

Josie's father remembered the hospital chaplain apologizing, five years earlier, "What you're about to be offered isn't *ideal*. I wish I could do more than give you a choice between two bad options. But at least it's a choice."

Now he swallowed hard and told Josie, despite the ache in his throat, "This is what's best for you." He hoped he sounded firm, not on the verge of tears. He quickly added, "And I'll visit. Every chance I get."

Josie's father tugged her into the hallway and shut the heavy wooden door behind them. One of the shadows ahead of them separated from the wall and began gliding toward them. It made Josie's father think of ghosts and ghouls, but Josie boldly stepped forward and called out, "Hello! Are you the Nice Lady?"

The shadow replied with a deep chuckle, "You're welcome to call me that."

"Let us see your face," Josie's father called. "Your eyes. I have to know that I can trust you."

"You trust me," the shadow said calmly. "You're here."

The shadow came close enough that Josie's father could see that it was a small woman wearing a severely plain outfit: black turtleneck, black blazer, black pants, black shoes. She also wore a black veil over her face. The woman reminded Josie's father of a mourner at a funeral, and even five years after his wife's death, that felt right to him.

It also felt right for this particular night.

"I remember your voice," he said.

Many times in the past five years he'd wondered if he'd imagined the entire conversation with the mysterious woman the hospital chaplain had summoned. Or maybe he'd misunderstood. The woman had stayed in the shadows that night, too—and he'd been too tear-blinded to see well, anyhow. But he remembered the kindness in the brown eyes, the patience she'd had with his grief-stricken stupor. She'd said that everything he needed would be sent to him. She'd said he wouldn't need to commit absolutely until Josie was ready to start kindergarten.

What parent, holding a newborn, ever fully understands how quickly a baby turns into a kindergartener?

But the packages had started arriving only a few weeks later. Their contents were so simple in the beginning: wooden blocks and cardboard books. Later, there were bigger, fancier books with elaborate pictures that Josie's father took to peering at himself at night, long after Josie was asleep, because they were so beautiful. And there were museum tickets and swimming lesson vouchers and videos of wondrous places Josie's father had never even heard of, that Josie would need to pretend she'd visited for real.

And as Josie's father devotedly followed the instructions that came with every package, the books and the videos and the museum trips raised new thoughts in his own head, too.

Leaving a museum where they'd seen Egyptian mummies and Peruvian gold and Chinese calligraphy—and a computer chip the size of Josie's thumbnail, but capable of launching a trip to Mars—Josie's father said to her, "We're part of that world, too, Josie bean. We're connected to all of that!"

And Josie said, "Why wouldn't we be?"

And Josie's father was glad that she didn't know answers to that question. He was glad that her world would always be bigger than his had ever been.

You knew this was coming, too, he told himself now, staring at the dark hallway narrowing ahead of him. It felt like he was becoming the ghost—the one growing paler and paler; the one about to fade away into nothing, without Josie. But still: *You knew this was always about Josie, not you. Don't be greedy, trying to keep her to yourself.*

"Come," the shadowy woman beckoned them.

She led them down a flight of stairs, and then down again.

"You'll sleep here, Josie," the shadowy woman said, pulling out what seemed to be a drawer. "Go ahead. Look inside."

Josie poked first her head and then her whole body over the rim of the drawer. But her father reeled backward.

"They look like . . . like coffins," he choked out. "This could be a crypt!"

"They look like charging stations," the woman corrected. "They *need* to look like charging stations. From the outside. But, see . . ." She touched a release inside the drawer, and its back panel fell away. No—Josie's father bent down to look more closely—the back of the drawer had unspooled into a charming spiral of stairs.

With a muffled whoop of glee, Josie immediately slid down the banister.

A light followed her, down and down and down. Dimly, Josie's father realized this effect was only because of motion sensors; it wasn't literally a matter of all the light in his life leaving alongside Josie.

"The lights are uniquely attuned to Josie's genetic makeup," the shadowy woman murmured. "This space will belong solely to her."

Now Josie's father could see: Inside the drawer, beneath and behind the false back, was a cozy little room with a tiny bed and a braided rag rug.

Josie landed squarely on the bed, and giggled and bounced.

"She'll outgrow that," her father protested. "Even by first grade, this space will be too small for her."

"Every summer the other whatnots will be sent away for updating, and the storage areas will be rehabbed in their absence," the woman said. "As Josie grows—and as the other whatnots *look* like they grow—they'll move up to larger charging stations. And Josie will move into a larger room."

Josie's father racked his brain for another loophole, something the woman hadn't thought of that would mean he could still turn around and take Josie home with him.

"Won't the kid notice when all his 'friends' go away at

once?" he asked. "The boy, I mean, the one whose parents are paying for all the whatnots?"

"He won't notice," the woman said. "Because we'll time the updating and rehab to coincide with the boy's own vacation with his family."

Josie's father barely knew the word "vacation." But the woman went on as if to explain: "And that's when you'll get to have Josie visit you for three weeks straight."

Josie's father had opened his mouth to protest again, but now he abruptly shut it.

The woman glanced over her shoulder at a clock on the wall.

"Josie will need a good night's sleep to be ready for tomorrow," she said.

Josie's father gulped.

"Josie, sweetheart," he said weakly. "Remember everything we talked about? Remember how I said the time would come when I'd have to go away?"

"You promised not to cry, Daddy," Josie said, sounding as strict as a five-year-old possibly could.

"I'm not crying," he said.

He wasn't yet, anyway.

"I'll be good and brave and smart and kind," Josie said, as if she'd memorized her lines. "I'll learn everything I can. And then I'll grow up and come home and take care of you."

She'd made up the last part herself. That wasn't what he'd told her.

"No—you'll grow up and take care of *yourself*," he said. "Because you'll be able to, then."

"We'll take care of each other," Josie murmured, snuggling into her blankets. "We always do. Even when we're not together."

Josie's father swallowed a lump in his throat. He bent over and kissed her forehead.

And then there was nothing left for him to do but tiptoe out.

ELEVEN

Josie Before Max—Six Years Ago, and Counting Down to Their First Meeting

That night, after Josie's father and the mysterious woman went away, Josie *meant* to quietly burrow deeper into the blankets and fall asleep until morning. She meant to follow every single one of the mysterious woman's instructions.

But she was five years old, and she was in a new, exciting place she'd never seen before, that just called out to be explored.

And she was Josie.

She closed her eyes and *tried* to summon sleep. But she could hear the mysterious woman's footsteps fade away; she could hear the click of the lock two stories up when the mysterious woman left.

She had the entire school to herself.

Josie had never been alone before. Her father's apartment was only one room, so when she was home, she'd always had him with her. And when he was at work, she'd always gone to a neighbor lady's apartment, where Josie was just one of a dozen toddlers and preschoolers who argued and fought and made up and fought again over broken crayons and ripped books and dolls that were missing arms and legs and hair, and toy trucks that were missing wheels. And the neighbor lady presided over the hubbub by being able to yell louder than any arguing or crying child. She was also louder than the sirens wailing outside or the laugh track of her TV shows hooting and hollering day and night.

Josie was used to falling asleep in noise, not silence. She was used to being crowded and jostled and poked and prodded and hugged.

Not ever left alone.

Alone is . . . scary, she thought.

But right away, her brain rebelled.

No—alone is an adventure! she told herself.

She sat up, and that motion made the light in her little cubbyhole room come on. For a few moments, she just played with this phenomenon: up—light on. Down—light off. Up, down, up, down . . . Josie giggled, and turned to ask her dad how the light knew to go on and off.

But of course he wasn't there.

And then Josie couldn't stay in the little room a second longer, just thinking about how her father wasn't there.

She scrambled out of the bed and up the small row of stairs at the side of the room. Then she pushed her way out of the drawer. In the dim glow of the security lights of the outer room, she walked around pressing her ear against one drawer after another, listening for the hum of the android whatnots recharging. She admired the way the recharging could sound so much like human children breathing—it made her think of naptime at the neighbor lady's day care, the times when she woke up and everyone else was still asleep. It made her feel simultaneously cozy and itchy to move. She could have crawled into one of the other drawers and cuddled up with one of the other whatnots—the *real* android whatnots, as she reminded herself; the whatnots who were supposed to be whatnots. Probably everything would have turned out differently if she'd opened one of the other drawers. But she had *alone is an adventure* ringing in her brain now. She could explore the whole school building, top to bottom; she could test out the toys in the classroom; she could play on the playground all night long, if she wanted to. . . .

Josie fell asleep that night draped over a globe in the second-grade classroom, and the next morning she woke up barely in time to dart back down to the basement before the janitors came in to scrub away her muddy footprints. (She'd attempted cartwheels between the playground swing sets, because she'd never before seen so much space for playing; she'd gotten mud on her hands, too, trying to do handstands beneath the monkey bars.) If the janitors wondered how foot-prints could appear in a supposedly empty school building in the middle of the night, they kept their questions to themselves. They were very well-paid janitors, and they seemed to understand that they were being paid for their silence as much as their cleaning skills.

But by the light of day, Josie felt like she already knew the school inside and out; she was a kindergarten expert. She knew the alphabet and she could read a little and she thought of counting like a game; she was like a thirsty sponge that could soak up every drop of learning that might ever come her way. She was primed.

So when she walked into the kindergarten classroom, she wasn't worried. She wasn't scared.

She was just the tiniest bit lonely; she was bursting to tell *someone* about the wondrous things she'd discovered.

Fourteen children—or, rather, fourteen child-shaped creatures—sat in a ring on rainbow-colored carpet squares. Thirteen of them sat quietly, peacefully, contentedly—as if they existed only to sit.

The fourteenth kid bounced and squirmed and gawked, spinning his head side to side, looking now at the alphabet letters in the ice-cream cone on the wall, now at the faces drawn on the numbers between one and nine being held up by puppies and kittens on the giant poster at the front of the room. He had swirly brown hair that made Josie think of pinwheels, and rosy red cheeks that made Josie think of apples. His wide-set eyes made him look perpetually surprised and excited.

This kid looked like he would appreciate knowing which swing on the playground swing set had the squeakiest chain, which hallway water fountain sent the water in the highest arc, and which seat in the school library had the best view of the stars pasted on the ceiling overhead. Josie dashed over to sit beside him. She'd already opened her mouth to share all her discoveries with him when she remembered: She wasn't supposed to tell anyone that she'd spent the night at the school. She was supposed to pretend to be a robot pretending to be an ordinary kid. Almost everything real about her life now was supposed to be secret.

She was supposed to spend her whole day every day lying.

But she wanted to share *something* real with this other kid.

It was a good thing Josie's mind worked fast. She went with the one thing she'd found in common between her old life back home with her dad and at the neighbor lady's day care, and her new life here at this shiny, glitzy school:

"I like jumping in mud puddles. Do you?"

TWELVE

The Narrator's Aside—A Detail Josie Won't Find Out
for Years

The instant Josie crawled out of her drawer the night before her first day of kindergarten, an alarm went off in another underground room. That room was filled with screens showing footage from dozens of security cameras planted throughout the school.

One of the three guards monitoring the screens sent a text on a secure cell phone: We have a climber.

The reply came instantly: Which one?

Number twelve. Josie.

Crying? Screaming? Weeping hysterically for her daddy?

Not that I can see. Not yet. Just . . . exploring.

Keep an eye on her then, but don't intervene unless you have to. Follow protocol.

Got it.

The security guard thought that might be the end of it, but another text message popped up a moment later: Do me a favor. When you can do it secretly, go in and change the seating chart in the kindergarten classroom. Make sure Josie sits next to the boy.

Three dots bounced on the guard's cell phone screen, as if the cell phone itself was pondering Josie's fate. Then five words appeared:

She could be the one.

THIRTEEN

The Next Six Years

Josie grew up. Or I guess we should say: Josie *and* Max grew up. Together.

You probably think that sounds simple—after all, that's what kids do—but it never is.

In Josie's case, growing up meant having all sorts of odd things start feeling normal.

Sleeping in a basement.

Seeing her father only three weeks a year.

Having to lie to her best friend again and again and again.

That first day of kindergarten, it was easy. When Max and Josie ate applesauce and cheese crackers for morning snack, there was nothing in the world for either of them but that applesauce and those cheese crackers. It felt like there was no past and no future. When Josie started nibbling the cheese crackers into shapes—stars, moons, flowers, hearts—Max laughed and clapped and tried his hand (er, *teeth*) at turning his cheese crackers into bunny faces and diamonds. He didn't ask "Where'd you learn that?" and so Josie didn't have to make up any stories that erased the dirty, squabbling children she'd known at her old neighborhood day care.

It is a great thing to be five.

By the end of that first day, when Josie and Max drew a picture together of a swimming pool full of magic fish, the teacher looked down at their two heads bent together over the same paper, his curls blending with her wispy tufts. Josie had a green crayon clutched in her left hand and Max had an orange crayon clutched in his right hand, and they were adorning the scales of the same fish, alternating the colors without even needing to discuss it. The teacher said, "Well, aren't you two peas in a pod," and this already felt true.

So at the end of the first week, when they'd been insepVerable the whole week, it made perfect sense that Max told Josie on Friday afternoon, "My mom's going to call your mom or nanny or whoever to see if you can come over and play tomorrow afternoon."

Josie knew she couldn't tell Max, "I don't have a mom or a nanny." Her dad, who called her every single night, had said again and again, "You need to keep everything secret so you can keep going to that school." She'd thought that keeping secrets would just feel like obeying her father—*protecting* him, maybe, because what if the police arrested fathers who told their daughters to act like robots pretending to be kids?

What if the people in charge thought it was like Josie was stealing her education?

But staring back into Max's dancing eyes, Josie also felt that she needed to protect *Max*. He would be so sad for her if he knew that Josie didn't have a mother. Josie had seen Max get tears in his eyes over a book about a bird with a broken wing—he would probably cry if he knew that Josie's mother had died.

So Josie wrote down the phone number of the mysterious kind lady and slid it across the table and said, "This is who your mom should call." And then she started talking about whether they should play with Legos or act out "Goldilocks and the Three Bears" with stuffed animals next.

She told herself she hadn't really lied.

But this was her first untruth. Her first evasion. By the time they were in fifth grade, Josie felt like she was drowning in them.

So she and Max were best friends, yes.

But they weren't exactly equals.

You might even argue that he didn't know her at all.

FOURTEEN

Now—Max Seeking Josie

No matter what anyone tells you, I'm real.

Max read the note again. Real? Of course Josie was real. She was the most real, vivid person he knew. Next to her, every other kid he'd ever known might as well be a cardboard cutout. Even the people he loved most besides her—his parents and Nurse Beverly—were just background noise, occasional blats and blurps, while Josie was the symphony that sang through his every waking moment. Every time he arrived home from school and Mom or Dad or Nurse Beverly asked, "How was your day?" his every sentence began "Josie said . . ." or "Josie thinks . . ." or "Josie and I . . ."

So why would Josie leave this note for him? Why would she think she needed to write down such an obvious fact?

Max reached for his phone again. He looked at the unanswered text, **Can you talk?**—still unanswered—and he called her anyway.

After all the ringing, her voice burbled out: "You got Josie! Well, not actually, because you really just got my voicemail. But leave a message, and I'll call you back!"

"Call me. Even if it's the middle of the night," Max said. "No matter what."

He knew Josie would if she could. And that meant that every second that passed without her calling convinced Max more and more that something was wrong.

"Max! Dinnertime!" Nurse Beverly called from outside his room. "Shut off your computer and go on down to the dining room."

Max closed his laptop lid and tucked his phone into his pocket. He raced down the stairs, kissed both parents on their cheeks, and slid into his seat beside the long, long table that was scaled for grand entertaining, not a mom and a dad and a boy having a simple meal together. Distractedly, he glanced at the table full of food—they were having swordfish again—and then he pulled his phone out of his pocket and glanced at the screen once more. It had taken him two whole minutes to run down the stairs, and maybe he'd accidentally had the ringer turned off and so he'd missed a call from Josie.

Nope. She still hadn't called or texted back.

"Max, please," his mother said. "You know the rules. No phones at the table."

"Yes, but—"

His mother held out her hand and Max obediently slid his phone into it. She ruffled his hair as if to soften the scolding. Then she stood up and carried the phone into the kitchen.

Max's mother was one of those women who just always looked pretty. He'd gotten his curly hair from her, as well as the dark eyes that could seem to dance with excitement. But more than that, Max knew that she was deeply, deeply kind. She was as likely to cry over a broken-winged bird as he was.

So he knew he could have said, "Mom, I'm worried about Josie. She told me something weird." And Mom would have talked it all out with Max. She would have insisted on calling Josie's parents or nanny or *someone* to make sure that Josie was fine.

But would she really? Max wondered suddenly. The first few words of Josie's note came back to him: "No matter what anyone tells you . . ."

Would Mom make sure that Josie was fine, or would she just make sure that she could tell *me that Josie is fine?* Max wondered.

Only a day before, he would have trusted his mother completely. But now . . .

Now he had to find his own answers.

Max's father's phone rang just then, and he immediately answered it.

"Sterling here," he said, motioning to Max and Max's mom

that they should go ahead and start eating. He slid his chair back from the table and went into the next room, muttering, "But we've got time before the Tokyo markets open—"

"*Dad's* allowed to have his phone at the table," Max observed, unable to keep the bitterness out of his voice.

"Oh no, Max. You're only eleven," Mom said. "Please don't tell me you're turning into a snarky teenager already!"

She hugged his shoulders from behind, taking the sting out of her words.

"I know it seems like a double standard, but your father needs to stay in constant contact with his business interests," Mom added apologetically, slipping back into her chair. "He really does wish he could get a break from work. Or have a job like mine, where it's possible to set limits."

Max's mom ran an art museum—she was often on her phone for that late at night, too. But at least she didn't miss dinner.

Max watched his father pacing back and forth in the living room. Dad smoothed his hair down and grinned and said, "No, no, it's good you called. Here's what we should do."

He didn't look like he regretted anything.

And somehow that made it so that when Max got his phone back after dinner—and Josie still hadn't called or texted back—Max knew he had to do something.

I'll find her, he told himself. *Now. I'll go to her house.*

His heart pounded with the daring of this idea.

Somehow, in all their years of being friends, they'd never played at Josie's house. It wasn't something Max ever really wondered about. He had so many, many toys himself, and so many places for them to play at his own home—not just in the swimming pool, but also on the family tennis courts, in the home gymnasium, on the miniature racetrack with the kid-sized cars that had belonged to Max's dad when he was a kid. . . . If Josie invited Max anywhere, it was to visit the public library or to go for ice cream or to watch a movie in a theater that was quaintly open to everyone (or, at least, everyone who could pay), instead of at the private home-viewing theater that Max had in his own house. And they also saw each other when they took tae kwon do and tennis and golf lessons, when their school won a computer-coding championship, when they played in a youth orchestra that brought kids together from all over the city. (Josie and Max both chose to be percussionists.)

They just never hung out at Josie's house.

Still, Max knew where Josie lived. He'd known since kindergarten, when Josie had excitedly told him about a new piece of playground equipment they'd get to play with at recess.

"I saw it when I was brushing my teeth before bed, and it surprised me so much I accidentally spit toothpaste at the mirror!" she'd laughed.

Back then, Josie just wanted to talk about how the new

playground equipment could shoot basketballs high up into the air. So Max didn't say, "Oh, you live so close to the school that you can see the playground out your bathroom window?" But that fact had lodged in his brain with everything else he knew about Josie.

Max, in kindergarten, had been fully in agreement with Josie that basketball-shooting playground equipment was much more interesting than any other topic.

And somehow the topic of where Josie lived had just never come up since then.

But Max knew that there was only one house whose windows overlooked the school playground. Sometimes when he and Josie were swinging on the playground or racing around the playground track or dangling on the playground climbing wall, he'd glance over and see one of those windows and think, *Is that Josie's bathroom? Is that where she stands to brush her teeth?*

But there were always other things to talk about.

Could I get the chauffeur to drive me to school tonight? Max wondered now. *Can I say I forgot a book or a T-shirt or something like that, and then when I'm pretending to look at the school I can sneak over to Josie's house instead?*

That wouldn't work. If Max said he wanted to check the school lost-and-found, Mom would say it wasn't fair to make the chauffeur go out at night when Max could easily wait until morning.

Or—until he got back from vacation and camp.

Then I'll have to sneak out on my own, after everyone's asleep, Max told himself. *I'll have to do this alone.*

Max had never done anything alone.

He texted Josie once more: **Are you okay?**

It was agony watching the screen of his phone and *not* seeing it light up with any reply. It was agony having to say "Uh-huh" and "Hunh-uh" to Nurse Beverly as she went through the checklist with him after dinner to make sure he had everything packed for vacation and camp.

It was agony waiting until she left and Mom and Dad went to bed, so Max could sneak out without anyone seeing.

And it was agony wondering, *Am I brave enough to do this? Can I do this without chickening out?*

At midnight, lying in bed, he heard Mom's light, tripping footsteps on the stairs, and then the more imposing thud of Dad's footfalls. And then, when he could hear nothing but silence outside his room, he sat back up.

He was brave enough to do this. He was doing it.

He had to know about Josie.

He took his bike, and managed to sneak past all the overnight security guards by walking it through the woods at the bottom of the hill. Outside the gates of his family's estate, the world looked completely different. The familiar, gently winding boulevard he traveled every day in his family's limousine was darker and more grimly shadowed than he'd ever seen it.

That's only because you've never been here at midnight before! he told himself.

Maybe after he saw Josie—after he found out for sure that she was fine—her mom or dad or chauffeur would be willing to drive him home.

He reached the block with the school and the house he thought of as Josie's, but both buildings were almost unrecognizable in the dim light from the streetlamps. And there were odd shapes on the sidewalk between the buildings—was it just end-of-the-school-year garbage that hadn't been picked up yet?

Wasn't that kind of . . . trashy?

"The sign says 'Free to a good home—anyone is welcome to take this'!" he heard someone call from the other side of the odd shapes.

Quickly, Max darted into the shadows beside the front steps of the school. He pulled his bike after him, and crouched down, watching ten or twelve people descend upon the pile of trash.

"Gotta love it when rich people move and leave all sorts of good stuff behind," someone else chortled.

It's just leftover garbage from school, and these people think it's "good stuff"? Max marveled.

He wanted them to get whatever they were looking for and

go away, so he could go knock on Josie's door. He peeked out again just as a particularly scrawny-looking young man—little more than a teenager, really—held up a lamp and cried out, "Look at this! Good as new!"

And . . . Max recognized that lamp. It had a glass shade with rainbow-colored butterflies around the rim. Some of the butterflies even had flecks of glitter on their wings, as if someone had wanted to make it even brighter and more dramatic.

Max had seen that lamp in a picture. It had been at the beginning of fifth grade, when their teacher had had them take selfies to illustrate an essay about "My favorite place to read." The picture had gone along with the best essay in the class, about how great it was to read snuggled up in bed, in the glow of a bedside lamp.

Josie had written that essay. Josie had taken that selfie.

And that was Josie's lamp.

FIFTEEN
Now—Max Panicking

Max stretched out even farther to peer up at the windows of the house he thought was Josie's. All the windows were dark.

Not just "It's after midnight and all the lights are out" dark, Max thought. *That looks like "Nobody lives there anymore" darkness.*

Or "My best friend moved and didn't even tell me" darkness.

The leftover garbage on the sidewalk had to be from Josie's house, not the school.

Josie's *old* house.

Max yanked his phone out of his pocket.

Josie! Did your family move? Why didn't you tell me? Is that why you said we might not go to the same school next year? WHERE ARE YOU? YOU HAVE TO TELL ME!

And then a second later, there was the most blessed sound Max had ever heard: a ping. The words flooded across the phone screen.

I'm so sorry—we did move. I was mad about it so I didn't

want to tell ANYONE. I wasn't even looking at text messages. But this doesn't change anything about where I'll go to school next year. Really, I'm fine. Everything's fine. You go have fun on vacation and at camp. We'll see each other when you get back. If you want.

Max blinked at the message on his phone screen in confusion. Later, he'd try again and again to sort it out: *Josie's fine? That's good news! I don't blame her for being mad about moving, but at least she won't go to a different school . . . except she doesn't say it's the same school as me, does she?*

And what does she mean, "if you want"? She knows I'll want to see her! Why would she write that? How could she write that?

I . . . I don't think Josie wrote that. . . .

For now, though, he'd only gotten as far as, *Josie's fine? That's good news!* It was late and he was tired after swimming all day, and it was scary to be outside after midnight in the dark, so close to people picking through trash. And he *wanted* to believe that Josie was fine.

He wasn't used to anything going wrong.

A second later, relief flowed over him when he saw his family's familiar limousine pulling up at the curb, right beside the front steps of the school. He'd felt so daring, sneaking away from home in the middle of the night. But now it was wonderful to see the sleek black car with the STERLING #1 license plate. It was heavenly to think of sliding in onto the soft leather seats and just going home. In no time at all, he'd be back in his own cozy bed.

The door of the car sprang open, like a summons. Max scrambled in, pulling his bike behind him. There was plenty of room. After he shut the door, he just had to prop the bike up, so the pedals didn't rip the seat.

Max looked through the spokes of his bike's front wheel, ready to thank the chauffeur for coming for him. He was ready to say sheepishly, "I guess I didn't do such a great job of sneaking out. I guess the guards saw me, after all."

But his mouth froze, half-open, as soon as he saw past the bike.

It wasn't his family's chauffeur in the driver's seat.

It wasn't anyone he'd ever seen before in his life.

SIXTEEN

The Narrator's Aside

You see how there would have been so much scrambling behind the scenes, don't you?

You know there had to have been security sensors all around the Sterling family's property, so no one could sneak in or out. You already know the school had all sorts of security cameras and guards watching over it. Max couldn't have crouched down beside the school stairs without being observed.

There wouldn't have been a minute of Max's journey when he was ever truly alone.

He hadn't had a single moment in his entire life that was like that.

He also hadn't had a moment in his life when he had to stand up for what he believed or think completely for himself or defy anyone who thought they could tell him what to do.

Yet.

SEVENTEEN

Josie the Same Day, Only a Few Hours Earlier

"SpaghettiOs!" Josie's father exclaimed, bringing a battered pot to the kitchen table and lifting the lid. "Your favorite!"

"Thanks, Dad," Josie said, forcing herself to beam up at him. "You're the best."

Every summer when Josie went home to see her father, she felt like she was wearing funhouse glasses the first day or two. Everything she looked at—the SpaghettiOs, the splintery table, her plastic bowl, her father's face—seemed like an eye test. Or a brain-and-heart test. *Were* SpaghettiOs still her favorite food, or were they nasty, wormy-looking globs of starch in watery sauce that could be appreciated only for being cheap? Was the plastic bowl sweet and adorable because it looked like a woven crown around the rim, and Josie could still remember using it to pretend to be a fairy-tale princess when she was three or four? Or was it ugly and disgusting, because it had been left too near the stove once, and so its side was scorched and melted and distorted, and it should have been thrown away years ago? (Except, then what would she eat out of?)

Looking into her father's face was the hardest. He was still her hero, the one who loved her most, the one who'd given up everything for her—even given up seeing her, except for three weeks out of the year. But there was always a moment that first day after she arrived home when she'd peer into his eyes and . . . she couldn't see *him* at all. He would look like just another down-on-his-luck laborer in a patched shirt and worn jeans, one with broken teeth and a crooked nose and mournful eyes and a stark line between white skin and sunburn, whenever he took off his cap.

The first time that had happened, the summer after kindergarten, she'd seen everything spin around right again as soon as her father grinned at her. He'd swept her up into his arms and whirled her around the apartment, and it had instantly become a wonderful, magical place where she was deliriously happy once again. And he'd turned back into the strongest, most handsome, smartest, *greatest* daddy any little girl had ever had.

After that, most years the first few days after coming home were like having an eye doctor constantly switching out the lenses covering Josie's eyes: *A or B? What's in focus, and what's gone blurry now?*

Which way would you rather see?

And then she'd make the switch, and she'd feel like she could see fine until she went back to school and she had to adjust in the opposite direction there.

But so far today, she'd only ever gotten glimmers of seeing her father as he truly was. The melted plastic bowl hadn't looked like a crown even once. The splintered table looked more rickety than ever.

And Josie was afraid she'd gag if she had to put a spoonful of SpaghettiOs into her mouth.

It's because of Max, she thought. *Because I'm not sure I'll ever see him again.*

And because I broke the rules. I told. Which . . . might ensure that I'll never see him again.

Josie slumped in her chair (which was just as rickety as the table). She dropped her spoon.

"You know what?" she asked. "I had a lot of food at our end-of-the-school-year party. I don't think I'll be hungry until tomorrow. Why don't you eat my share?"

Dad's eyes flashed, and he quickly tilted his head down.

Oh no! He is hungry, but he doesn't want to let me see that he really wants my food. . . . Or is he insulted? Does he think I think I'm too good for SpaghettiOs now?

This was new, too: Josie thinking she could almost read things in Dad's face that he didn't want her to see.

Almost.

Dad put the lid back on the pan, and slipped it into the refrigerator. The kitchen was so small that he could do that without even standing up from the table.

"Tell you what," he said. "We'll keep the food until later then."

Josie had just made things worse. Now Dad would stay hungry until she could pretend she wanted the SpaghettiOs.

But when Dad turned back from putting the pan away, he caught Josie's eye.

"Hey," he said. "You don't have to worry anymore. You did it. This came in the mail today and . . . I didn't think you would mind if I opened it right away. I was going to celebrate with dessert, but *I* can't wait for you to get this news if we're going to postpone dinner. The past six years are paying off!"

He slipped a thin envelope into her hand. Josie pulled out an elegantly embossed sheet of paper. She barely skimmed it before dropping it on the table.

"You think I'm going to be excited because . . . I've been invited to take some exams?" she asked. "Dad—I just *finished* taking exams! I'm done with school for the summer!"

Her throat ached, thinking of everything else she was done with. *Seeing Max every day. Having my own room. Having a library right there in the school with me, so I could read all night if I wanted to. Being able to text Max anytime I wanted, anytime I had an idea I wanted to share with him . . .*

Even now, she found herself automatically reaching for her phone, because she wanted to tell Max, "My dad wants me to take more tests! Can you believe it?"

But her hand closed on empty air. She'd had to turn in her cell phone when she'd left behind everything else at school—everything that wasn't really *hers*, but belonged to her only when she pretended to be a whatnot. So she wouldn't even know it if Max texted her.

Who could say what the Whatnot Corporation might tell him, pretending to be her?

Her dad laughed.

"You didn't read the whole letter, did you?" he asked. "I guess I hated tests when I was a kid, too. But, Josie, you're good at them! And these tests"—he pointed to the letter lying open on the table—"they're going to earn you a scholarship! Look at all the good middle schools you're going to be able to get into. And you'll be able to go without keeping secrets, as *yourself*, living right here at home with me the whole time. . . . That's what the last six years earned you. You got enough education that you're going to ace those tests! You'll get to be at some big fancy school as yourself!"

Josie snatched up the letter again and eagerly read the list of schools.

"Penobscot," the school Max would be going to, wasn't one of them.

But her dad was still beaming, his face a sunrise of hope.

"I do want to stop pretending," Josie mumbled. "I do want to live with you."

Josie may not have figured out yet how to get her eyes to work right again, but she could hear perfectly well.

She could hear exactly how much she'd failed to sound excited—and failed to make her words sound true.

And surely her father could hear that, too. He wasn't stupid. All she had to do was look him straight in the face, and she'd see the death of all that glorious hope he'd been holding on to for the past six years.

After six years of pretending, couldn't I have managed it even one more night? she wondered. *For one more sentence? For Dad?*

She still loved him, just as much as ever. She knew how much he loved her, how much he'd sacrificed. But after six years of having to divide her heart for more than eleven months out of every year—of having to force herself to wall away all her longing for her father, because that was what *he* told her she had to do—she needed more time to recover.

And to recover from leaving Max behind.

Rather than look her dad in the face and see how much she'd hurt him, Josie glanced out the kitchen window.

And what she saw outside made her bolt up from the kitchen table and run out the door.

EIGHTEEN

Max in the Limousine After Midnight

The person in the driver's seat wore black. She—*Or maybe he? No, she*—was so thoroughly covered in dark clothes that Max at first wondered if she was just a shadow, just a shape.

Kidnappers are like that, Max thought. *Kidnappers try not to be seen.*

He untangled his arms from the bike he'd pulled into the car and grabbed for the door handle. His suddenly sweaty hands slid right off.

Locked. Of course it's locked, just like always. . . .

He'd just opened his mouth to threaten, "I'll scream! Everyone will hear me!" when someone else spoke first.

"Max, save your questions until you get home," someone said. "Your parents are waiting for you there."

It was Nurse Beverly, sitting on the passenger side of the front seat. But she'd turned around to peer at Max in great concern.

Max leaned his head back against the leather seat and took

in deep, relieved gulps of air. Nurse Beverly would never be involved in a kidnapping.

"I thought, I thought . . . ," he burbled. A new idea swam into his mind. "Am I in trouble? I can explain."

Nurse Beverly always had a kind look in her eye when she gazed at him, but now she radiated so much compassion and concern Max could have drowned in it.

"Max, I'm sorry," she said. "It's not really my place to discuss this. You'll be home in a minute or two."

The shadowy driver stayed silent. But the car crept forward, leaving behind the people picking through the trash on the sidewalk—the people picking through *Josie's* trash.

But where's Josie? Max wanted to ask.

Maybe his parents were preparing some sort of surprise for him. Sure, it was the middle of the night, but somehow Josie was also still awake. Her text proved it. Maybe she'd told her parents about how upset she was, and about how Max had sent her a worried text message. And now maybe Josie and her mom and dad had gone over to Max's house, and talked, and Josie's parents were agreeing that Josie should go to school with Max next year. And not just that, but Josie would go to camp with Max. And who knows, maybe because Max and Josie had had so much upsetting them, all the parents would say, "We feel so bad for you. Why don't we let Josie go along on Max's vacation, too?"

Everything in Max's life had a way of turning out right.

That whole scenario seemed possible. Maybe even likely.

But when the limousine pulled up in front of Max's house, he could see only Mom and Dad waiting in the doorway. They both wore tightly wrapped robes and the groggy, distressed expressions of adults who hadn't expected to be awakened.

The shadowy driver stopped and got out and opened the door for Max.

Then, to his surprise, the driver began climbing the towering stairs up to the house alongside him.

"Beverly, you stay, too," Mom called.

Max looked back: Nurse Beverly had gotten out of the car as well, but was heading off into the darkness, back toward the servants' quarters.

"I don't really think it's my place to . . . ," Nurse Beverly began.

"Please," Mom said. "For Max. And . . . me."

Max was not used to seeing Nurse Beverly looking uncertain or undecided. But she seemed conflicted now. Her feet still turned toward the servants' quarters, but she swiveled the upper part of her body back toward Max.

"All right," she finally said. "For Max."

What did it mean that she so clearly left out Mom? And Dad?

It was bothering Max more and more that he didn't know the fourth adult with them, the woman beside him on the stairs. The odd driver. Even when she stepped into the light,

he couldn't quite make out her face through the thick . . .
hood? Veil? Max wasn't even sure he quite knew the right
words to describe her clothes.

Camouflage? he thought.

The clothes were completely dark, not mottled, but their
purpose still seemed to be deception. Hiding.

The woman's face stayed a blurry smudge beneath her
veil. Max could tell only one thing about her: that she was
frowning.

"You don't have to do this," the woman told Mom and
Dad as she stepped in through the front door with Max.
"The revelation was contained. You can continue following
protocol."

"My son is old enough now," Dad growled. "He deserves
to know the truth."

Dad was looking Max straight in the eye, as he never
quite had before.

"We always promised ourselves we'd never directly lie to
him about this," Mom said, her flutelike voice sounding like a
trill of danger. "If we followed your protocol, we'd have to lie."

What was going on?

"Mom? Dad?" Max asked, the words coming out like
stumbles. "What are you talking about?"

Mom froze. Then she frowned, just as intently as the
mystery woman.

Mom never frowned at Max.

"I guess . . . I guess I never saw this day coming," she said. It sounded like an apology. "We should have prepared better."

Nurse Beverly quietly shut the door behind Max and the woman wearing all black.

"Son, we're rich," Dad said, placing a hand on Max's shoulder. "You know that. Because of my hard work. And because of my father's and grandfather's and great-grandfather's hard work. And sometimes when kids grow up rich, other kids get jealous. Other kids can be greedy and mean. They—"

"No, no, that's not why we did this," Mom said. "Or, not the main reason. Max, you know my life was very different from yours when I was your age. *I* didn't grow up rich."

Did Max know that? He tried to remember Mom's stories from childhood. But they were all about giggling with friends, and her parents singing lullabies, and how excited she'd been about going to school.

He couldn't remember any stories she'd told him about money, one way or another.

"I didn't want you to grow up thinking all you ever had to be was rich," Mom said. "I wanted other kids to be friends with you because you were a kind and wonderful person. Not because you had money."

"Parents can have multiple reasons for choosing to raise their children around whatnots," the mystery woman murmured. "Just because the reasons are different, they don't . . . cancel each other out."

"Whatnots?" Max seized on the unfamiliar word. He almost said, "Josie told me about them," but managed to choke back that secret at the last minute. "What are whatnots?"

"This is the make-or-break moment," the mystery woman with the hidden face said to Mom and Dad, as if Max wasn't right there listening. "You can still choose not to—"

"He's a smart kid," Dad said. "He's *my* kid. Of course he's figuring it out ahead of whatever schedule you think most kids would be on." Dad looked straight down at Max. "For your own protection, Max, all the kids you've ever known so far in your life—every single one—they've all been fakes. Machines. Robots. Uh . . ."

Max had never heard his father falter so badly.

Max couldn't make sense of that. Or of what his father was saying.

"Androids," Mom finished for him.

She looked like she was going to either faint or throw up. She was watching Max so intently she seemed to be studying even the air molecules on his eyelids.

Nurse Beverly laid a hand on Max's shoulder. Because Dad's had slipped off.

"I'm sure this is a shock," she said.

"Er, yes," the mystery woman said. "You might want to take some time to adjust to this information. To fully grasp it."

Max's head spun. *All the kids you've ever known . . .*

Androids . . . The words lined up in his mind alongside the note he'd seen in Josie's handwriting: *No matter what anyone tells you, I'm real.*

"No," Max moaned, staggering backward. "No. That's not true."

"I'm sorry," Mom whispered. "But it is."

"No!" Max's voice soared into a scream. The words were exploding out of him. It wouldn't have been possible to stay silent, to keep everything bottled up inside. "You're wrong! There's Josie! She's alive! She's human!"

He figured out exactly what he wanted to say:

"She's just as real as I am!"

NINETEEN

Josie, with Her Own Discovery

Josie rocketed down the stairs of her apartment building. Her father's apartment was on the third floor, and there was no elevator. So she was just as used to climbing up and down stairs in the summertime as during the school year. But tonight she had no patience with them.

"Josie!" her dad called behind her, racing after her. "Where are you going?"

"I saw—" Josie was too out of breath to explain. "I'll tell you later. For now—"

For now, she had to get down to the street before the girl she'd seen was gone.

I'm probably wrong, it probably wasn't her....

But it certainly had looked like Ivy.

Of all the whatnots Josie and Max had gone to school with, Ivy was the one Josie noticed the most.

She was the one who seemed the least like a whatnot.

The first day of kindergarten, when Josie and Ivy were

both in the bathroom washing their hands before lunch, Ivy had looked over sideways and shyly asked, "What are you?"

And Josie was instantly shot through with dread. Could Ivy tell Josie wasn't really a whatnot? Had Josie already failed so badly at pretending to be a robot pretending to be a child that even a whatnot like Ivy had figured it out right away?

For once, Josie was speechless.

"I mean, what group are you in?" Ivy clarified.

"Oh," Josie said, as calmly as if she recovered from panic attacks all the time. "Eagle. Me and Max both."

The teacher had divided them all into groups with bird names, and every week a different group would get to "soar" down to lunch and recess first. That was all Ivy was asking about.

"You're an Eagle?" Ivy repeated. She sounded truly disappointed, not just machine-voice disappointed. "I'm a Dove."

Both girls looked down at their chubby, little-kid hands under the shared faucet. Josie's normally pale skin had turned a little rosy from the hot water, while Ivy's skin was so beautifully dark it made Josie think of the black velvet curtains in the school auditorium.

For a moment, Josie forgot everything she'd been told about pretending to be a whatnot. She just acted like a little girl who wanted to make a new friend.

Which was what she really was.

"You're pretty," Josie said. She beamed at Ivy. "And I like your barrettes. I like the little smiley faces on them."

"My mama gave them to me," Ivy said. "She—" Something in her face shut down. "It doesn't matter. You're just a whatnot."

Josie swallowed hard.

"Right," she said. "And you're just a whatnot, too."

Sometimes it was hard to remember that with any of the whatnots, but especially Ivy.

Ivy always drew the most beautiful artwork—her specialty was fairy-tale palaces covered in leafy vines that perfectly matched Ivy's name. In third grade, when everyone wanted to play tetherball at recess, Ivy was the reigning champion, and when Josie forgot herself and grumped, "I'll never be as good as you," Ivy said, with what sounded like true kindness, "It's only because I'm the tallest. You're actually better at jumping." And when they had to do social studies group projects with three people, Josie always suggested she and Max ask Ivy. Max probably thought it was just because Ivy was best at drawing maps and other illustrations. But Josie also liked how Ivy would sit there so quietly while Max and Josie ping-ponged ideas back and forth, and then when they ran out of steam, she'd speak up with the best idea of all: "So you want to act out that scene from history?" or "So if everyone else is writing about kings of England, we should do the queens."

Once late at night, early on in kindergarten, after Josie had already hung up from talking to her dad for the evening, there'd been a moment when the school felt unbearably big and quiet and empty, and Josie still felt too wide awake. And she'd crawled out of her little room and knocked on the charging-station drawer she knew belonged to Ivy. If Ivy had poked her head out, Josie planned to say, "I'm not really a whatnot. Let's pretend you aren't one, either. Let's just be friends. I can be friends with both you and Max."

But Ivy hadn't answered the knock that night, and Josie never tried again.

Because Ivy *was* just a whatnot. Ivy needed to spend all night every night cradled in the charging station, or she wouldn't be able to do anything.

Ivy is probably locked up in the charging station right now, back at school. Like all the other whatnots. Or back at the factory, being upgraded so she'll look even taller and bigger and like a sixth grader instead of a fifth grader . . .

So it was foolish that Josie was sprinting down the stairs.

But she kept going. She burst out onto the street and jerked her gaze side to side. The sidewalks were still crowded with workers like Josie's dad, just now arriving home from their jobs in other parts of the city. Parents carried hungry little kids who reached out for the gleaming apples and peaches of the sidewalk stands.

And then, above the crowd, far down the block, Josie saw

a tall woman whose skin was the same deep, dark, velvety shade as Ivy's. Josie raced after her, dodging sharp elbows and jutting knees.

And there, beside the tall woman, was Ivy.

With one hand, Ivy was holding on to the tall woman's purse strap; with the other, Ivy was wiping a little boy's face. The little boy gazed up adoringly at Ivy.

And Ivy was transformed. The quiet, dreamy, well-behaved Ivy from school was chattering away excitedly to the tall woman, breaking off the words "—and then we learned—" the instant she saw Josie.

For a moment the two girls just stood there staring at each other.

And then Josie said, "You're not a whatnot. You were never a whatnot!"

Ivy stared back at her with wide, startled eyes, and whispered, "Neither were you."

TWENTY

The Narrator's Aside

Wait, what?

Ivy wasn't a whatnot, either? There were more real kids besides Josie pretending to be androids pretending to be kids?

Don't look at me to explain this. It's a surprise to me, too.

TWENTY-ONE

Back at Max's House . . .

"Max, I'm so sorry," Mom said. She had tears in her eyes. "We didn't mean to traumatize you. This isn't how I imagined this going."

She laid a soothing hand on his arm, and Max jerked away. He lost his balance and almost fell, kicking the wall in his effort to remain upright. That felt so good, he kicked it again.

"She's real!" Another kick. "Josie's real!"

"Stop that," Dad said, pulling Max away from the wall. He settled him down onto the couch. "Get ahold of yourself."

Max had never wanted to hit or punch or kick another person in his entire life. But he wanted to punch his own father now.

That confused Max, too.

He threw himself flat on the couch and sobbed into the pillows.

"And this illustrates why we tell parents to wait until their kids have socialized with other children like them, before revealing the truth about whatnots," the mystery woman said, above him. "It's easier to come to terms with outgrowing the shallow friendships of early childhood once they have more mature friendships."

Max understood every word she said—"friendship," "truth," "mature," even "socialized"—but it felt like she was speaking a foreign language. No, not just a foreign language, but a foreign language underwater. And backward and upside down.

"Oh, Max," Mom sighed. She sat beside him on the couch, a fact Max was aware of only because he felt the couch cushion dip down. She began stroking his hair, smoothing each individual curl.

Normally, Max loved it when Mom did that. But now this made him furious with her, too.

"This will make more sense to you later," Mom began. "But . . . think of the whatnots like training wheels on a bike. Only, they were like training wheels for friendship. You won't understand this yet—and I'm glad you can't understand this yet!—but real, human friends don't always treat each other as kindly as you and Josie do. People make mistakes. *Kids* make mistakes. Kids especially. They say and do hurtful things. They . . . they can break your heart. Childhood friendships can be so brutal. We didn't want you to have to go through that. And we didn't want you to learn bad habits, and start thinking it was okay for you to be mean to other kids, because that's what you saw them doing. . . ."

"So *you're* going to be mean to me?" Max wailed into the giant pillow on the couch. He turned his face to the side, appealing to Mom even though he was too teary-eyed to actually see her. "By taking away Josie? My best friend?"

"Max, please," Dad said. His voice seemed to come from far away. Farther than just across the room. "Pull yourself together. We already told you. She's not real."

"He's going to need some time to digest this," Nurse Beverly said, almost as if Dad were Max's age, and Nurse Beverly was scolding Dad.

"I don't see why you couldn't have a final meeting with Josie," Mom said, still stroking Max's hair. "To say goodbye. Or—"

"Actually, that is expressly forbidden in these circumstances," the mystery woman said, sounding as brisk and disinterested as if they were discussing drying paint. "Now that he knows the truth about whatnots. Surely you read the terms of the agreement when you signed it years ago?"

"But—" Mom began.

"Okay, fine—we'll get our attorneys to find the loopholes," Dad said, biting off his words. "We'll make arrangements."

Max liked that Dad sounded so fierce on Max's behalf. Of course Dad would fix this.

"There are no loopholes," the mystery woman said calmly. "No 'arrangements' like that would be allowed. To quote section thirty-two, line forty-five of the document you both signed, 'Once a child has been told about his whatnot upbringing, no further contact with the whatnots he was raised with shall be allowed.'"

How could Mom and Dad *not* be able to fix this? How could they have signed such a horrible contract?

How could any of it matter if Josie wasn't real?

She's real, she's real, I know she is. She has to be, we have to stay friends. . . .

Max rose up from the couch.

"Stop it!" he roared. "Stop talking, all of you! Stop saying I can't see Josie! Just . . . leave me alone!"

But that wasn't really what he wanted, either.

TWENTY-TWO

Josie, Questioning

Josie and Ivy were still standing stock-still on the sidewalk, staring at one another in shock, when Josie's dad caught up with her. He'd evidently run after her the whole way down the stairs and along the street—she hadn't been paying attention, but apparently he'd been shouting, "Josie! Josie! Wait!" the entire time.

He was out of breath.

"Dad, this is my friend Ivy," Josie said. The word "friend" just slipped out. "I didn't know she lived near us. But . . ." What she wanted to say to him was too big to put into words.

"A friend? From . . ." Dad panted.

"From *school*?" Ivy's mother asked, her eyes widening.

If Josie hadn't known any better, she would have said Ivy's mother was afraid. But what was there to be afraid of?

"I signed an agreement," Dad said to Ivy's mom. "Did you sign an agreement?"

Still wide-eyed, Ivy's mom nodded.

"This isn't allowed," Dad said. "We'll get in trouble. We'll lose everything." He began tugging on Josie's arm.

"We'll stay off this street from now on," Ivy's mother said, her eyes locking on Dad's. She started pulling on Ivy's arm, too, pulling her and the little boy away from Dad and Josie.

The crowd swirled around them, creating eddies and islands. It wasn't just that Dad and Ivy's mom kept yanking Josie and Ivy in opposite directions; the currents of the crowd seemed to want them apart, too. But just before they lost sight of each other, Ivy darted her head forward and whispered in Josie's ear: "Fifteen-eleven Sawfallen Street, apartment six-oh-one. She leaves for work at noon. Every day."

"Are there more of us?" Josie whispered back. *More whatnots who aren't really whatnots,* she meant.

Between the crowd and the pull of Josie's dad and Ivy's mom, Josie and Ivy were too far apart now to be able to whisper after that. With the hubbub of the crowd around them, they were too far apart to be sure of hearing each other even if they shouted. So in the last moments before they lost sight of each other, Josie had to resort to reading Ivy's lips.

Still, she was certain she understood: Ivy was whispering back, "We have to find out."

TWENTY-THREE

The Narrator's Aside

Whew! I am back on solid ground here, with all this talk of agreements. I've read them now. I've examined the fine print. I know what I'm talking about this time.

Max really isn't allowed to see Josie ever again.

Josie and Ivy really aren't allowed to meet outside of school.

But . . . we both know that Josie doesn't always follow the rules.

And Max will, uh . . .

Huh. Maybe I still don't know what I'm talking about.

TWENTY-FOUR

Josie, Deciding What to Do

"Study hard today," Dad said.

Josie blinked groggily up at him. It was the next morning, and Dad was headed off to work. She was still snuggled on her mattress on the floor, and Dad was tucking his own blanket around her shoulders for extra warmth.

"I still can't believe I'll get to see you every single night from now on," Dad said. "For once I won't have to give you back after three weeks."

"Yeah . . . ," Josie murmured drowsily. "Have . . . a good day at work."

"I think you're talking in your sleep!" Dad laughed and patted her cheek. "That's okay. It's still so early. You're a kid. You can sleep late, now that we don't have to take you to day care."

That was another big change this summer: Dad had decided Josie was old enough to stay home by herself while he worked.

Josie snorted.

"I get to sleep late *and* study hard?" Josie asked. "How can I do both at once?"

"You know what I mean," Dad said.

Josie could hear the traffic on the street outside—lots of early-morning laborers like her dad were already headed off to work. But he stayed crouched by her mattress a moment longer.

"Josie, I didn't get a chance to study," he said. "When I was your age, I was already working all the time. My family needed the money. I was picking up rocks, pulling up weeds . . ."

"Before you started building castles in the air," Josie said loyally. This was an old joke between them. Her dad often did work high above the ground, sometimes even trotting across exposed beams in half-built skyscrapers to fix problems left behind by automated cranes. That had enchanted Josie when she was little. But it scared her now.

"And I know your stories, Dad," Josie said. "I . . ."

She was supposed to thank him for everything he'd done for her. For the fact that she *didn't* have to work all the time. And if everything worked out, she would never have to risk her life for a paycheck like he did. She wanted to thank him. But she didn't want to say words that were just words, that weren't heartfelt. And her brain was still too scrambled for that.

Max . . . Ivy . . . Dad . . .

"You know what?" she said. "I don't think I'm awake yet.

This is all a dream, right?" She flipped over onto her back and made a big show of pretending to be sound asleep and snoring like a chain saw.

"Yes, you get to have dreams," Dad said softly. "Not nightmares."

Josie kept her eyes tightly squeezed together.

Tell him thank you, she told herself. *Say it like you mean it. Say it. Say it. . . .* But the undercurrent of *But what about Max? What about Ivy?* still thrummed too strongly in her brain.

When she finally opened her eyes again, Dad was already gone.

She hadn't told him thank you. But she also hadn't flung the angry words at him that were simmering below the surface: *How could you and Ivy's mom have signed those agreements? How could you have promised things about who I was allowed to talk to, what I was allowed to say, where I was allowed to go?*

How could I not go visit Ivy today?

All morning, she made bargains with herself.

I'll be careful. I don't have a cell phone anymore, so no one could track me electronically. . . . I'll wait until after noon, so Ivy's mom couldn't get in trouble either. . . . I really will study this morning, so I'll make Dad happy, too. . . . I'll still get into a good school like Dad wants, no matter what. . . .

As soon as the local library opened, she went there and dutifully pulled the dullest-sounding books off the shelves—*Study Prep for Citywide Sixth-Grade Curriculum, Middle School Entrance Examination Reviews*—rather than the storybooks that called to her instead. But she also sat down at one of the library computers and called up a city map.

Let's see, 1511 Sawfallen Street. . . .

She'd just put her hands in position to type the apartment building number when she thought to look around. The library was packed, and nobody seemed to be peering in her direction. But a little dome hung from the ceiling alongside the old-fashioned fluorescent lights.

It was probably a security camera. Dad had pointed out security cameras to her once at a museum they'd gone to when she was little. He said that was how the disembodied voice knew to come on with the warning, "You are standing too close to the artwork. Step back, or you will be asked to leave." And he'd said, "They're probably watching us in particular. Because we aren't dressed right. We don't talk right. We don't belong here. But . . . you'll belong here when you grow up. You'll fit right in."

She hadn't understood at the time. She hadn't understood that he'd really been saying "We're poor. Everyone else here is rich."

Everyone else in this library branch was poor, too . . .

and that was why the library computers were all guarded by security cameras. That was the only reason.

But Josie pulled her hands back from the computer keyboard. She stood and then walked up and down the rows of old bookshelves instead, until she came to an ancient book labeled "City Maps." It took a long time to look up Sawfallen Street in the index, flip to the proper page, and memorize directions without so much as touching her finger to the page. But it seemed safer. Wiser.

Promptly at noon, she got up and left the library. She walked twenty blocks. When she got to Ivy's building, she didn't go in the front door. She walked around to the back, and pulled a garbage can over to the bottom of the fire escape.

And then she began to climb.

She was really only looking for an open window, a route into the building. But when she got to the sixth floor, hands reached out one of the windows and pulled her in.

It wasn't just two hands. It was four.

TWENTY-FIVE

Max, Deciding What to Do

Max woke up in the morning with swollen, puffy eyelids from crying so much the night before. This had never happened to him before, and at first it confused him.

Why are my eyes so hard to open? I'll have to tell Josie about this!

Oh. Josie.

Everything from the night before flooded back. According to Mom and Dad and the strange mystery woman, Josie was something called a whatnot. An android. No more real and human and—and *herself*—than a stuffed animal or a toy.

Or an imaginary friend.

According to the adults, Josie basically *was* an imaginary friend.

"Of course the two of you got along great," Dad had said. "All those whatnots, they were programmed to be like the kind of kids you needed around you most. Your mother and I, we *paid* to have them designed and programmed that way."

"And they were supposed to be as realistic as possible," Nurse Beverly had said, more gently. "So you shouldn't feel embarrassed about being fooled."

"I'm not *embarrassed*!" Max had protested. "I'm mad! Because you all lied to me! I mean, you're lying to me now!"

He'd felt like he was spinning out of control, like he might do or say anything.

If the adults could say such ridiculous things, he could be ridiculous, too.

"That's enough," Dad had said, like he was closing a business deal. "We're trusting you with grown-up information. You do *not* accuse us of lying. Act like you deserve to be treated as an adult. There are all sorts of secrets we kept from you when you were a little kid, all sorts of little fantasies we let you believe. As you grow up, you're more ready for the truth. That's how life works. You didn't cry like this when we told you there wasn't a tooth fairy. This is the same kind of thing. Take it like a man."

Now Max felt a new tear squeeze out of his eyes. He heard a rustling over by his drapes. A flood of light splashed over him—Nurse Beverly must have come in and opened his drapes and blinds just like she did every morning. She was probably about to say, "Rise and shine!" her usual greeting.

"You're going to tell me it's time to get up," he said sulkily. "You're going to act like it's any other day, and not, not . . ."

Not the morning after I lost my best friend. The morning after everyone told me my best friend isn't even real.

Max felt a cool hand on his forehead. He squinted up into the too-bright light temporarily blinding him.

"Go tell Mom and Dad I'm not going on vacation with them," Max said. "Tell them I'm staying here until they bring Josie back."

Someone crouched beside his bed. It wasn't Nurse Beverly— it was Mom.

"Oh, Max," she said, brushing his hair back from his forehead. "I don't think any of us are in shape to leave on vacation right now. Or to enjoy it. We're postponing the trip."

"You are?" Max sat up. Maybe he would get everything he wanted. "And Josie—"

Mom shook her head.

"Max, I feel terrible about this, too," she said. Her hand shook, and she dropped it to her side. "Terrible about how everything happened, what a bad job we did telling you . . . maybe even about the decision we made nearly twelve years ago, to raise you around whatnots at all."

"Twelve years ago?" Max asked, his voice cracking. "You're saying even the kids I knew in preschool were fake?"

Mom stared down at her knees, folded under her.

"When you put it that way . . . Max, we really were trying to help you," Mom said. "We really thought this was for the best."

She patted his hair again and then, oddly, scrambled up and left the room.

Was *Mom* crying?

Max lay still for a moment longer, until it became unbearable. Automatically he reached for his phone to text Josie. He wanted to tell her, "Mom is acting so weird"; he wanted to ask, "What do you think I should do to get my parents to let me see you?"

But last night, the last text he'd gotten from Josie had been weird, too. It hadn't sounded like her. She was real—she'd told him that herself. But her text hadn't sounded real.

He tapped out a cautious, hesitant message:

Hello? Josie? Are you there? Where are you? What are you doing? What do you know about . . . things?

The answer came quickly:

This phone number no longer belongs to Josie West. All questions about Josie West must be directed to the Whatnot Corporation. Office hours are Monday through Friday, 9 a.m. to 5 p.m.

Max dropped the phone as if it had suddenly turned red-hot.

You'd think they'd at least keep pretending if . . .

No. Josie's existence hadn't been pretending. He would have known. He would have been able to tell if she'd been fake. All those years they'd spent together—all the secrets they'd whispered in each other's ears, all the games they'd played, all the texts they'd sent, all the school projects they'd assembled—everything they'd done together made him an expert on Josie West.

She. Was. Real.

Max sat up, energized. He'd go back to the school. Josie's things had been left by the curb—he'd find an address, if the trash pickers hadn't taken everything. He'd break into the school if that was what it took to track down Josie.

He sprang up and ran out of his room. Halfway down the long second-floor hallway, it came to him that he might be behaving a little strangely. It would have made sense to change out of his pajamas.

So what? he thought. *I don't care.*

But it seemed like a good idea not to let Mom or Dad see him.

When he reached the stairs, he went from running to tiptoeing. Down on the first floor, he was just about to pass the breakfast room when he heard Mom's voice. He flattened himself against the wall.

"Yes, I'm upset, too!" she was saying. "I feel like we totally messed this up. We should let Max see his friend one last time."

"Friend?" Dad said. "It's a *machine*." But then even his voice turned sad and soft. "I already called our attorney. But . . . he says the contract we signed is airtight."

Mom sighed.

"Maybe . . . Maybe we need to expose Max to other

friends," she suggested. "New friends."

"You mean, more whatnots? Or real kids?" Dad asked.

Max wanted to storm into the breakfast room and scream, "Josie *is* real! And one friend isn't just replaceable with another! People aren't interchangeable! They're not like, like . . ."

Like robots.

Max doubled over, too much in pain to move, let alone scream at anybody. He let out a whimper that was so soft no one could hear him.

"Max isn't going to be fooled by whatnots anymore," Dad said. "And if you think he should meet up with other kids who already know the truth about whatnots, that would be seventh graders. You want your son, who's upstairs crying right now, hanging out with seventh graders? I was a seventh grader, once upon a time. They'd eat Max alive."

"You were a seventh grader before the invention of whatnots," Mom said weakly. "Seventh graders who were raised with whatnots—they'd be nicer."

A clink sounded from the breakfast room, as if Dad had put down his fork a little too hard.

"I bet kids still act like kids," he said. "Seventh grade— ugh. Worst year of my life."

"And we're going to put Max through that?" Mom sounded like she was on the verge of crying again.

"Sounds like it's either that, or put him into a hermetically sealed box for the next four or five years—I'm joking, I'm joking!" Dad said. "Look, I know last night was awful. I have emotions, too. Though, of course, seventh grade taught me how to hide them. . . . And I'm not proud of how I acted when we told Max everything. 'Take it like a man'? 'Grow up'? It's like I opened my mouth, and my father's voice came out. But Max *is* going to have to toughen up. It's a dog-eat-dog world out there. I know you don't always see it, because you want everyone to be nice, but—"

"I run an art museum," Mom said, her voice icy now. "*You* may not value what I do, but I deal with all sorts of people with gigantic egos and equally gigantic insecurities. I deal with you when you say ridiculous things like 'Take it like a man.'"

Were Mom and Dad fighting now? Because of Max?

They never fought.

Or maybe he'd just never heard them fight before. Maybe that was something else they'd always protected him from.

"We wanted Max to grow up with the kind of confidence that comes from always being around family and friends who love him," Mom said, her tone turning plaintive. "Have we undermined that completely?"

"*No*," Dad said. "Max is still going to come out ahead. Because he found out about whatnots at the end of fifth grade, not sixth, he's going to have more time to adjust than the other kids do. The way to look at disadvantages is, how can this be turned into an advantage? Max has gotten used to being the top dog at school, because he's always had that. He'll have that in middle school, too. We've set him up for success, just like we wanted. Just like any parents want for their kids."

Once again, Max wanted to scream at his parents. Or maybe just at his dad: "I'm not a dog! I'm not going to adjust to any place that's dog-eat-dog! I won't toughen up! And *I* don't care about succeeding! I care about Josie!"

But all he could do was stay doubled over, whimpering.

He *really* needed Josie now. Josie would know how to solve everything.

TWENTY-SIX

Josie, Surprised

It was Ivy hauling Josie in through the sixth-floor window of the apartment building—Ivy and another girl who looked so much like Ivy that Josie at first thought they must be twins. Then, the two girls straightened up and faced Josie directly, and Josie realized that the other girl was even taller than Ivy. She was more grown-up, too—more like a version of Ivy that was somehow a few years older.

It took Josie a moment to understand.

"You have a sister?" Josie gasped to Ivy. "It's not just you and . . ."

She looked around for the little boy who'd been with Ivy and her mother the night before.

"My brother, Casper, is napping," Ivy said, easily understanding. "He'd tell on us for sure if he saw you here, so we put him down to sleep as soon as Mama left for work."

She pointed toward a closed door off to the side. The existence of a second room meant that Ivy's family had a bigger apartment than Josie and her dad did. But this place was just as run-down. The fake wood of the floor here was just as cracked as the tile at Josie's; the walls were just as battered as the ones Josie and her father scrubbed again and again without ever getting rid of the stains. And the ceiling was so full of water spots that Josie could easily imagine Ivy staring up at them at night and pretending, as Josie had done in her own apartment as a little girl, *Is that a bunny or a bear? A pig or a porcupine?*

"Ivy said you'd be prompt," the other girl muttered. Her voice was both deeper and richer than Ivy's—and more sarcastic. She even rolled her eyes. "Whatnot training, right?"

Josie thought about her dad telling her, again and again, "You have to be on time for everything, when you're at school. No—you always have to be early. Or else someone will figure out that you don't belong."

She also remembered him reading directions to have her sit alone in a room, staring at a marshmallow, while he timed how long she could go without eating it. And then he had thrown away that packet, muttering, "No. Some things are just too cruel."

"I don't think Josie got the same training we did," Ivy said. "She never acted like . . . us."

Josie's brain wasn't working right. This was like being in one of those dreams where she kept trying to add up a row of numbers, and when she woke up she realized half of them weren't numbers at all, but nonsense symbols. Or the dreams where she was sitting in class, and everyone else was speaking a different language that Josie didn't understand.

At least Josie understood the *words* Ivy was using.

"You said 'we,'" she said to Ivy. "And 'us.' Does that mean your sister was someone who pretended to be a whatnot, too?"

"I'm Lucinda," the older girl said. "Don't you dare call me a whatnot."

Bewildered, Josie looked to Ivy for help.

"She thinks it's a bad word," Ivy said. "Calling someone a whatnot is like saying they don't matter."

"Or they matter so little, they're interchangeable with androids," Lucinda said bitterly. "With machines. The whole system, taking poor kids away from their parents, saying the only way they can get a good education is if they pretend to be androids—it's all rotten. It's *wrong*."

Josie kept watching Ivy.

"So, because of having a big sister, you knew everything all along?" Josie asked. "Way back, that first day of kindergarten when you and I said to each other, 'You're just a whatnot'—you knew even then that not all the other whatnots besides you were robots?" She didn't know if Ivy remembered that conversation from the first day of kindergarten or not. "You knew from the very beginning who was human and who wasn't? Except, I guess, you didn't know about me. . . ."

What if there was a group of kids in our class that got together every night at school and had fun while I was eating dinner alone and counting the minutes until I could call Dad? Or just hoping Max would invite me to his house to play?

Josie felt an unexpected lump in her throat. But this time, it wasn't because she missed Max.

"*No*," Ivy said. "Lucinda didn't know the truth about whatnots, either, back when we were in kindergarten."

"I went to school with a rich kid named Ashley," Lucinda said. "Starting in preschool. I thought Ashley and I were the only real kids, and everybody else was fake. I mean, it made sense. We were both Black girls—we were so much alike. We *matched*. I didn't find out everything until after the end of fifth grade. Until I was the same age you and Ivy are now."

Fifth grade, Josie thought. *When I got the letter left in my cubicle, telling me I may or may not be going to the same school as Max next year . . .*

"So how many of the other kids in your class were like you—and like Ivy and me? How many of the supposed 'whatnots' in the class with you and Ashley were actually real humans?" Josie asked.

Lucinda snorted, which made her seem a lot less like Ivy. Ivy's face was dreamy and soft and kind—even now, Ivy looked like she was imagining artwork in her mind, like she was studying the play of light on everyone's face. She always seemed to be looking around for beauty. Even though the tiny room around them was shabby and plain—suffocating, even—Josie had no doubt that Ivy could draw it in a way that would make it look like a palace, and make Josie and Lucinda look like princesses.

Meanwhile, the very bones of Lucinda's face were more sharply etched, her jawline more set. Her dark eyes were angry now, not kind, and her mouth twisted bitterly.

"I thought Ivy said you were really good at figuring things out," Lucinda scoffed at Josie. "She said you were smart. Do I have to spell everything out for you?"

"Maybe?" Josie squeaked. Was this what all older kids were like? Should Josie worry about heading off to middle school in the fall, regardless of whether she got to be with Max?

"Luce, don't be like that," Ivy pleaded. "Remember how you felt when you were a fifth grader? When you found out everything?"

And just like that, Lucinda's face went soft.

"Okay, I'll just go ahead and tell you both the truth," she relented. "Here it is: Everything you were told about whatnots was a lie. Of course it's a lie. How could anyone make androids so much like a real human being that even a self-absorbed rich kid wouldn't know the difference? Especially when they're together for years and years and years in class and on the soccer field and at slumber parties and standing beside each other in choir. . . . Technology isn't that good. Or—humans aren't that simple."

"What?" Josie gasped, even as Ivy muttered, "But that would mean . . ."

"Right," Lucinda said. "Every single kid in your class was truly human. Every single 'whatnot' you know was just pretending to be a machine."

TWENTY-SEVEN

The Narrator's Aside

What?

What?

WHAT?

Seriously, I never claimed to be an *omniscient* narrator exactly, but I really did think I knew the *basics* of the story I've been telling. I prepared for this! Truly I did! But now . . .

This puts all those agreements I read and studied in a totally different light. Let me look back . . . uh-huh . . . yeah . . . okay . . . Well. Let me look back at some of the earlier conversations we overheard, too. . . .

Do you have any questions?

I don't know about you, but *I* do. I have some things to find out.

Like, don't you wonder who the shadowy lady really is? You know: the woman who showed up to talk to Josie's dad the day Josie was born. Was she the same person as the "mystery woman" who drove the car to pick up Max the night his parents told him the truth?

(Er . . . what they thought was the truth but was actually a lie?

Is it still a lie if people think they're telling the truth but they don't actually know the truth?)

Anyhow, the shadowy lady had to have known the truth all along.

But why doesn't she want anyone else to know?

Why didn't anyone tell *me*?

And look back at what happened during Josie's first night at school. The first night she climbed out of her cubicle and went exploring. Don't you think it was the shadowy lady texting back and forth with the security guard?

Whoever it was wrote that Josie "could be the one."

What did *that* mean?

Does Lucinda know?

TWENTY-EIGHT

Lucinda Tells All. Or, at Least, Everything She Knows.

"Why didn't you tell me yesterday that all the whatnots were actually humans?" Josie asked Ivy. "Or—as soon as Lucinda told you?"

But Ivy had whirled on her sister.

"Lucinda! Why didn't you tell me that ever before?"

"Wait—you didn't even tell your own sister?" Josie asked Lucinda. "Until now?"

Not having siblings herself, Josie only knew about brothers and sisters from books. She had the impression that a sister would be the best thing ever. Someone who would stick up for you. Someone who would play with you anytime you wanted. Someone who would braid your hair and protect you from bullies and lie to your parents if she had to, to keep you out of trouble.

But Ivy hadn't had her sister with her her entire life. Starting in preschool, Ivy and Lucinda had each lived in separate cubicles in separate schools, both of them pretending—separately—to be whatnots.

Lucinda took a step back.

"It's been a rough year, okay?" she said. "I had my own problems. Ivy, remember, you were already back at school before I came home last summer. Before I got the letter telling me I . . . didn't get into any middle school with any rich kids." She looked down, as if she was ashamed. "And then at school, it took a while for everyone to sort themselves out. It was almost spring before anyone whispered to me, 'Have you heard of whatnots? I had to pretend to be one.' And then I had to decide 'Do I dare to tell the truth, too?' We all figured it out together. And then, if we tried to talk about it with our parents, they'd just look scared, and tell us to keep it secret."

"But you could have written to me," Ivy said, betrayal still painted across her face. "You could have texted, you could have called. . . ."

Lucinda stared down at her hands.

"I thought about it," she said. "But I was so confused. I imagined you drawing pictures in your cubicle at school— I always think of you drawing pictures—and every time I imagined you, I saw you with a smile on your face. I saw you being happy. I thought if I told . . . I'd just make you as confused as I felt."

"But if Ivy had known . . . If Ivy had known . . ." Josie

couldn't quite finish her thought. She gave up on talking to Lucinda, and turned to Ivy. "I used to pretend sometimes that you were just as real as me. I used to play this game at night, after Max went home and all the whatnots were plugged into their charging stations. Er . . . after all the other kids were in their cubicles? I'd go out on the playground alone. But I'd imagine that you were a real girl like me, and you'd come out to play, too. And we would swing together, we'd go down the slide together. We'd just *be*."

"Me?" Ivy said. A pleased smile teased at her lips. "You *wanted* me to be real?" Then her smile faded. "You probably thought that about everyone."

"Well, sure," Josie admitted. "But you most of all."

She could picture everyone from their class going out on the playground at night, as if that could have happened. Walking out together, tall Ivy would tower over Maddy, who was tiny and blond and blue-eyed. Jack, who had more freckles than anyone else Josie had ever known, would head for the basketball court alongside Xu and Serena. Cole and Caden would start shouting about choosing up teams even before they'd figured out what game they wanted to play. Sona, Ryan, Kendall, and Omar would haul out the jump ropes.

Why did it seem so different to imagine everyone on the playground at night, than how they were on the playground at recess during the day?

Because during the day, I only ever paid attention to Max. I barely even looked at the others.

Was that only because she and Max were best friends?

Or because she'd always thought of everyone else as a whatnot?

TWENTY-NINE

The Narrator's Aside

You think I've got any behind-the-scenes information to share with you now? Any more security guard text exchanges with the shadow lady?

Sorry, no.

I can tell you that Josie's efforts to evade the security cameras in the library and then on the way to Ivy's apartment didn't work very well. Sure, Josie avoided letting the security cameras near the computers at the library record her looking up Ivy's address. And, yes, by going around to the back of Ivy's building, Josie avoided being caught on any security camera set up near the front door.

But there are security cameras *everywhere* in Josie's and Ivy's neighborhoods. Josie's actions were picked up on all sorts of cameras.

But no "shadowy lady" or any of the Whatnot Corporation security guards have seen any of that security footage. Not yet.

None of them know what they should be looking for.

They're still watching Max.

THIRTY

Still Josie and Ivy

"Let's start over," Josie said. She held out her hand to Ivy as if they'd just met. "Here's what I should have said that first day in kindergarten: Hi. I'm Josie. I'm having a lot of fun today. I like all the toys in our classroom. And the playground. But I had to sleep here in the school building last night. And I *really* miss my daddy."

Ivy giggled and shook Josie's hand.

"Ivy," she said. "I've been spending every night at one school or another ever since I was three. First it was in a preschool for a boy named Cardiff. Then for a girl named Emerson. Now it's kindergarten for Max."

"He was still Maximilian that first morning," Josie corrected.

Ivy shrugged and tilted her head side to side, like she was deciding.

"What I've learned is . . . you have to be quiet and well-behaved," she said. "*Perfectly* well-behaved. Or else they kick you out. That's how come I started drawing all the time. Every time I wanted to run or jump or step out of line or let go of the knotted rope we always had to hang on to in preschool, I'd think about something to draw. I didn't mind sitting down all the time, if I got to draw. And when I was drawing, I'd forget how much I missed my mommy and my big sister, Lucinda."

"No, no, no," Lucinda said, waving her hands at them. "You don't get do-overs. You're not kindergarteners anymore. If you two talk like that in middle school, everyone will make fun of you."

"I won't make fun of Ivy," Josie said. "And Ivy won't make fun of me. Max wouldn't make fun of us either."

She crossed her arms and stomped her feet like a little kid signaling, *so there.*

Ivy giggled again. Josie had never heard her laugh so much.

"That just . . . isn't how things work," Lucinda said. "You and Ivy won't get to go to the same school."

Josie's stomach clenched. What if she didn't get to go to the same school as either Max or Ivy?

This was odd—she and Ivy had barely spoken to each other over the past six years, outside of class. But Josie would miss her if they weren't at the same school.

"How do you know?" Josie challenged Lucinda. "Maybe we'll all get to stick together. Maybe our whole class will. That would be so great!"

Now she held her hand up, and Ivy high-fived her.

"You don't know Josie," Ivy told her sister. "Josie stepped out of line all the time, and they never sent her away. She was a bad influence on Max"—Ivy put "bad influence" in air quotes—"and the teacher never stopped her from laughing too loud or shouting out 'Ooo, this is so great! I just figured out the answer to the hardest problem. Did anybody else get this one?' when we were supposed to be taking math tests. And her reports . . . even when we were only supposed to talk for a minute or two about the book we read or the science facts we'd learned, Josie would get all excited and go on and on and on. Only Max was supposed to be allowed to do that."

"Is that true?" Lucinda asked.

"I guess I do talk a lot," Josie admitted. "I mean, I did. At school."

She'd just thought that the other kids didn't feel as strongly as she did about the ending of *The One and Only Ivan,* or about the fact that sharks average fifteen rows of teeth in each jaw, or about anything else.

Because they were whatnots.

Come to think of it, she hadn't done very well pretending to be a bland, boring, well-behaved whatnot. Everyone else in the class had been much better actors and actresses.

"That doesn't make sense," Lucinda said, sinking down onto the battered couch. "Nobody's allowed to be a bad influence on the rich kid." She studied Josie's face in a way that made Josie think that her hair might be sticking up, and she might have dried toothpaste lurking at the corners of her mouth. Then Lucinda turned back to Ivy. "Are you *sure* Josie wasn't the rich kid in your class, instead of Max?"

"Ha, ha—*no*," Josie said. She turned the empty pockets of her shorts inside out and held them up by their bottom seams. They had holes in them. She was back to wearing ordinary clothes because she'd had to return all her school uniforms. "I'm not a rich kid."

"Then why," Lucinda asked, "were you allowed to act like one?"

THIRTY-ONE

Max, in Agony

Nurse Beverly found Max still doubled over in the hallway.

"Breakfast will make you feel better," she said, sliding her arm around his shoulders, to steer him around to join his parents.

"No, it won't!" Max snarled, even though he never snarled at Nurse Beverly. "*Nothing* will make me feel better!"

He slipped out from under her arm and took off running. He forgot he'd planned to go to the school. Instead, he dashed back to the stairs and scrambled up them. He didn't stop until he'd gotten back to his room, and thrown himself across his bed. He buried his face in his pillow and went back to sobbing. Behind him, he heard Mom, Dad, and Nurse Beverly all cry, "Max?"

But only Mom and Nurse Beverly followed him. Max could hear them conferring outside his bedroom door.

"What are we supposed to do?" Mom asked.

"It's so hard seeing him in misery like this," Nurse Beverly said. "This was easier when he was a baby, and a good nap or a warm bottle was the answer to almost everything."

"Give him some space," Dad called up the stairs. "Boys his age—I mean, *kids* his age—they don't like being hovered over all the time."

Is that true? Max wondered.

Was it possible to want to be hovered over and want to be left alone—both at the same time?

Max waited, but no one came into the room to tell him what to do. After a while, he must have fallen asleep just from the sheer misery of crying. Because, the next thing he knew, the room was dim again, as if someone had drawn the drapes. And the angle of the light coming in through the cracks made him think it was afternoon now. He sat up, and saw that a tray was on his bedside table with some sort of meal contained under a silver dome. It must have been there for a long time, because the crystal glass of ice water beside the silver dome was speckled with thick beads of condensation.

"I'm not hungry," Max muttered. "If Josie isn't really alive and can't really eat, I won't eat either."

"I always wondered how that worked."

It was Nurse Beverly's voice. Max turned—she was sitting in the overstuffed chair near his bed. She might have been there for hours, maybe even longer than the tray of food. She was knitting what looked like a baby blanket, and it spread across her whole lap. The last time Max had seen her with that blanket—only the day before—it had been barely more than a thin strip of twisted yarn.

"Oh yeah—I saw Josie eat all the time!" Max exclaimed. "We learned about that in science. Only living things eat! So that proves she was real!" It felt like a betrayal that he'd said *was*. He corrected himself instantly. "I mean *is*. She *is* real!"

Nurse Beverly nodded in a way that was not quite agreement.

"The first time you invited that child to come over to play, I watched her so carefully," she said. "I thought I'd be able to tell that she wasn't human. Especially when you had your snack together—I remember it was carrots and celery sticks and pretzels and hummus. I watched her chew and swallow and chew and swallow. . . ."

"And Josie did all that just fine!" Max exclaimed. He was sitting up straight now. Clearly Nurse Beverly was on his side. She'd help him convince his mom and dad they were all wrong.

"No, she didn't," Nurse Beverly countered. "She was a mess—just like you. She ate the carrots and celery and pretzels like any five-year-old, forgetting to close her mouth when she chewed, and getting a little smear of the hummus in her hair. . . ."

"See? See?" Max agreed. "That's what I mean!"

"Max, I looked it up afterward," Nurse Beverly said.

"Chewing and swallowing can be a mechanical process. And the whatnot designers—they created androids that *look* like they are eating and swallowing and digesting food like a normal human child."

"Oh," Max said, slumping again.

For a moment, there was only the sound of Nurse Beverly's knitting needles clinking together. Then Nurse Beverly said, "I don't know if this will make you feel better or worse, but I'd pretty much forgotten myself that that child wasn't truly a child, the same as you. It *is* hard to believe that she wasn't. And since I always had to pretend anyway around you . . . well, now that I can stop pretending, it feels like someone's died. And if that's the kind of loss I feel, then for you . . ."

Max's eyes flooded with tears again. Nurse Beverly understood.

Or—she understood how it would be if Josie truly were just an android. But Josie wasn't.

"How can I prove, how can I show . . . ," Max began.

Nurse Beverly stopped knitting. Her eyes met his.

"You want proof, don't you?" she asked. She tapped the end of one of her knitting needles against her chin. "When someone dies, sometimes it helps when there's an open casket. It sounds terrible, like the last thing anyone would want, but it always puts me more at peace, to really see they're not suffering anymore, they're not in any pain, they're gone. . . ."

She seemed to be talking to herself more than to Max.

"Josie's not *dead*," Max said. He blinked, and the tears spilled out. "You're making this worse, even saying those words. And . . ."

Nurse Beverly stabbed her knitting needles into her ball of yarn.

"Your parents may have signed all sorts of agreements," she said. "But I didn't." She stood up, dropping the blanket, the yarn, and her knitting needles to the floor. "Come on."

THIRTY-TWO

Back at Ivy's . . .

"Don't you want to find out everything now?" Josie asked Ivy.

"I just *told* you everything," Lucinda protested. "Everything I know, anyway."

"Do you know where all the other kids from our class are?" Josie challenged. "Do you know if they know we're really human? Do they care? Do you know who first got the brilliant idea to make poor kids pretend to be robots? Do you know what's stopping any of us from just telling everyone the truth?"

"Don't know, don't know, don't care . . . but that last question, oh yeah," Lucinda said. "I know the answer to *that*. And you should, too. If you tell, you lose the chance to win any sort of scholarship for middle school. All the pretending you did—all those years being apart from your dad—that will have been for nothing."

This stopped Josie. She remembered the way her father had said, "The past six years are paying off!" His face had held such raw, naked hope when he handed her the letter about scholarships. Even if she didn't care herself, she couldn't ruin things for him. She'd studied all morning, hadn't she? Like her dad wanted her to?

"Okay, okay, I don't want to tell *everyone*," Josie said. "But Max—"

"—is a rich kid," Lucinda said. "He's already got everything he could possibly want, anyway."

"He was a very nice rich kid," Ivy said wistfully. "Not like the awful Ashley at your school, Luce."

Lucinda snorted and rolled her eyes.

"That Ashley," she muttered darkly.

"What's your favorite term for her today?" Ivy asked, with a teasing grin. "'Spoiled brat'? 'Poser'? 'Mean girl'? 'No-talent'? 'Wouldn't-be-anything-without-her-daddy's-money'?"

"Wait—you haven't seen this Ashley kid in a year, not since fifth grade, and you still have a new favorite insult for her every day?" Josie asked. "And you didn't even like her, or rich kids in general, but you're upset that you're not at a school with rich kids now?"

Lucinda dropped her gaze.

"I'm working through some things, okay?" She glanced back up, locking eyes first with Ivy, then Josie. "Look, I want all this to go better for you two than it did for me. But it's dangerous for you to be together, outside of school. Scrape together some money, buy a few burner phones so you can text each other without anyone else knowing—that way, you'll each start sixth grade with a friend, even if it's not safe for you to see each other ever again in person. Josie, you can even text *me* if you want. In secret. Everything has to stay secret. You can't go hunting up all the other kids from your old school just to find out what they do or don't know. You certainly can't go looking for your rich kid to spill the beans to *him*."

Lucinda's eyes flashed, and she looked angry again. But Josie saw the older girl's warning the way it was meant: as a kindness. Lucinda was offering to act like Josie's big sister, too. She was offering to let Josie and Ivy learn from Lucinda's own pain—from whatever Ashley did to hurt her, from all the misery Lucinda lived through during her sixth-grade year. Lucinda had learned lessons from all that, and she wanted Ivy and Josie to get the lessons without the pain.

But what if Lucinda had learned the wrong lessons? What if she still misunderstood, too?

"Ashley and Max aren't exactly alike just because they're both rich," Josie said. "Any more than the three of us are that much alike just because we're all poor. Or because we all had to pretend to be whatnots."

"Aren't they?" Lucinda asked. "Aren't we?" She waved her hand at Ivy and Josie, both sitting on the couch now, their shoulders leaned together. Lucinda let out a harsh laugh and shook her head. "The two of you have the exact same look on your faces right now. You both look like scared little rabbits—one black, one white."

Guiltily, Josie jerked her head to the side to peer at Ivy. Even with their differing skin colors, it felt like looking in a mirror: Ivy's eyebrows were arched just as high as Josie's own. And her eyes were just as rounded with surprise; the corners of her mouth turned down just as much as Josie's did. Josie remembered her kindergarten teacher calling her and Max "two peas in a pod"—now Ivy and Josie were the two peas.

But can't I be "two peas in a pod" with Max and Ivy both? Josie wondered.

Josie's head swam. This was much more confusing than the geometry she'd studied that morning, than all the stages of photosynthesis she'd memorized or the rise and fall of ancient civilizations she'd taken notes on.

"But I already—" she began, because she was ready to confess. She was going to tell Lucinda and Ivy about the note she'd left for Max under his laptop. The note he wouldn't see until he got back from his European trip and summer camp, because Max only used that laptop for studying, and Max wasn't one to study anything during the summer. It'd been a little bit of a gamble for Josie to leave the note there—she was gambling that no maid would find it first in the midst of overzealous cleaning; she was gambling that Max's parents (or maybe his new school?) would tell him about whatnots over the summer, and the note would be timed perfectly to let him discover the actual truth. And she'd gambled that her note was vague enough to seem innocuous if anyone else saw it, but specific enough for Max to understand.

Because she couldn't let him come to believe a total lie about her. She couldn't let him believe their friendship had meant nothing. Or that it—and she—were only make-believe.

But even as Josie tried to come up with the best way to explain all that to Lucinda and Ivy, Ivy dug her elbow into Josie's side. Josie was still peering at Ivy; Lucinda was staring at Josie. And Ivy widened her eyes ever so slightly and shook her head with the barest of motions and pursed her lips just enough that Josie could tell that she was trying to tell Josie something without Lucinda seeing. Was the word on Ivy's lips, *No*? Or *Don't*?

"Already what?" Lucinda asked.

"Come on," Ivy said, standing up and tugging on Josie's arm to pull her off the couch, too. "We've been talking a long time, and Casper's going to wake up soon. If he sees Josie here—even if he just hears her—and then he tells Mom, we're all in trouble. Luce, you'll have to ask your questions later. So will Josie. Josie, I'm going to write down my sister's cell phone number for you, so when you get a new phone, you can send your number to her. And she'll give it to me, so I can text you. And that's how we'll communicate from now on. Even if we're all three at completely different schools."

"Good idea," Lucinda said.

Josie let Ivy tug her toward the window, but she watched suspiciously as Ivy bent over papers spread over the nearby kitchen table. It had seemed a little too . . . convenient . . . that Ivy had suddenly gotten worried about her little brother waking up right before Josie could answer Lucinda's question.

Ivy kept her back to both Josie and Lucinda. Why was it taking her so long just to write down ten digits?

"Ivy, I know how you are," Lucinda chided. "You do not have to draw Josie an entire elaborate portrait along with my phone number."

"Yes, I do, if this is the last time I ever get to see her," Ivy said without turning around.

Josie got a lump in her throat, but Lucinda chuckled.

"My sister, the *artiste*," she said. But now she sounded proud.

The lump in Josie's throat grew until it felt too big to swallow. Lucinda and Ivy had each other. They also had a little brother and a mother. And for all Josie knew, they had a father as well, and grandparents and aunts and uncles and cousins. . . . Lucinda and Ivy would be fine, with or without texts from Josie.

For years it had been enough for Josie to have only her

father for family and only Max for a friend. That was all she needed. But now she couldn't quite get herself to see her father the way she used to. And Max . . .

Even if everything works the way I'm hoping for, it will be next fall before Max sees the note I left him, Josie thought. *Next fall before I'll know if he can stay a friend or . . . or I'll know for sure that I'll never see him again, either.*

A thin cry rose from the next room, followed by a child's voice whining, "Vy-Vy? Lu-Lu?" The handle of the door rattled.

"Oh no," Lucinda muttered. "He's learned how to open doors since the last time I was home. Josie, you've got to get out of here. Ivy, your masterpiece is going to have to stay incomplete. I've heard art's worth more money that way, anyhow. . . ."

With one hand, Lucinda began shoving Josie out the window. With the other, she yanked the page where Ivy was drawing out from under Ivy's pen. Without looking at it, she crammed it into Josie's hand.

"Sorry!" Lucinda hissed. "Just . . . don't let him see you!"

Josie barely managed to land on her feet out on the hot metal slats of the fire escape. Quickly, she flattened herself against the brick wall beside the open window so she'd be out of sight. She heard Lucinda's voice go unnaturally bright as she exclaimed, "Oh, Caspy! You're awake and ready to play again, huh? Let's go back in your bedroom and change your diaper first. . . ."

Clutching the paper with Lucinda's number, Josie lowered herself down the stairs.

She'd only gone one flight before curiosity got the better of her. Had Ivy sent her off with a portrait of Lucinda to go along with Lucinda's number? Or had Ivy thought Josie would want a drawing of herself? Or had she just embellished the numbers with her own namesake ivy trailing from every numeral?

Josie uncrumpled the paper. Then she flattened it against her knee.

Ivy hadn't drawn anyone's face. She hadn't drawn any ivy. Under the tidy parade of numbers beside the notation "L's #," Ivy had instead drawn a building. But it wasn't a palace or a castle or a fairy-tale peasant's humble abode—none of the types of buildings she usually drew.

It was their school.

And below the drawing, Ivy had written, I'll sneak out. Meet me there ASA . . .

Josie knew the last letter Ivy had run out of time to write.

It had to be a *P*.

P for possible.

THIRTY-THREE

Max and Nurse Beverly

Max didn't know where Nurse Beverly was leading him. But she certainly seemed sneaky about it. She crept down the stairs, pulling him along with her. Then she peeked all around before opening the front door. When they got out to the driveway in front of the house, she veered to the side. Maybe she was just seeking the shade of the tall oaks that lined the drive. The day was warm, and the afternoon sun was intense. But it felt more like she was aiming for the darkest part of the shade, the places where the shadows overlapped—the places where it was easiest to hide.

In fact, the way she scurried from shadow to shadow reminded Max of how he'd moved the night before.

"If we took a car, we could slump down, out of sight," he said, and instantly regretted how sulky he sounded.

"And if we took a car, the chauffeur would have to know where we were going," Nurse Beverly replied.

Max thought about complaining that he felt too light-headed

and dizzy to walk, because he hadn't eaten all day. He was probably in danger of fainting.

But he wasn't actually hungry. He didn't actually want Nurse Beverly to stop taking him wherever they were going and start fretting about how growing boys need good nutrition, and, here, let's get the cook to make you some nice chicken noodle soup or even just some Jell-O—little-kid food, little-*sick*-kid food. Max didn't want to be treated like a little kid or like he was ill.

But he did feel like a little kid right now. And he did feel even more head-spinningly awful than ever before, even worse than when he'd been truly in the grip of some disease.

He kept walking anyhow.

"Taking a little stroll," Nurse Beverly told the guards at the front gate. "Getting some fresh air."

They waved her on, and only nodded respectfully at Max.

Nurse Beverly made all the same turns Max had made the night before, walking past more trees and gently sloping parkland before reaching the scenic stretch of shops and townhouses. And then . . . the school.

"It's going to be locked," Max said, just as sulkily as before. All the trash was gone from the sidewalks now, and that made him feel even more as though he'd lost Josie forever. The school itself looked dark and empty and dead, the way schools always did in the summertime. But then a stunning thought occurred to him. "You aren't . . . you aren't going to try to break in, are you?"

They were already breaking rules, going to see Josie. Was he up for also breaking *laws*? Was he willing to become a criminal to get to Josie?

Yes, because she told me herself she is real—or, she wrote it, anyway—and this is how I'm going to prove it, Max thought. *And, anyhow, we could always explain to the police what we're doing, and why. . . . It's not like we'd be arrested.*

"Have a little faith in me," Nurse Beverly said, circling the school building toward an entrance at the back. "There are things that happen around you that you've never even noticed. There are *people* around you that you've never paid attention to."

"What does that mean?" Max asked.

"I just need to send a text," Nurse Beverly said, pulling a cell phone from the pocket of her voluminous tunic.

"Who are you texting?" Max asked. "That terrible woman from last night isn't going to find out that we're here, is she?"

"Don't worry," Nurse Beverly said. "It's not her."

She finished tapping away on her phone, then slid it back into her pocket.

And then a second later, the door in front of them buzzed and clicked open, separating a good inch from the doorframe.

"See?" Nurse Beverly said. "Nobody will know that we're here."

She pulled the door back farther. After the bright sunlight outdoors, Max was temporarily blinded peering into the dark hallway ahead.

"After you," Nurse Beverly said.

"But if nobody knows that we're here, who opened that door?" Max asked.

"You'll see," Nurse Beverly said.

Max felt more confused than ever. But he did have faith in Nurse Beverly. He did trust her.

He kept walking forward, straight into the darkness.

THIRTY-FOUR

Josie and Ivy, Reunited

Josie didn't have to wait until she got to the school before she saw Ivy again. Josie had just reached the subway platform at the stop nearest Ivy's apartment when she saw Ivy sprinting down the stairs from the street above. Josie waved her arms back and forth like a windmill to make sure Ivy saw her in the crowd. Ivy gave only a single curt nod. Then she meandered over to lean against the opposite side of the pillar Josie was standing by.

"Oh, you think we should avoid being seen together, in case there are security cameras?" Josie said, loud enough that her voice could carry to the other side of the pillar despite the crowd noise.

Josie heard Ivy sigh. Then Ivy scooted around the pillar until she was right beside Josie.

"We're going to walk into the school together," Ivy said. "I don't think it's going to matter whether anyone sees us together here or not."

"Then let's enjoy it while we can," Josie said. She held up her subway ticket. "I spent all my money buying this, so it's going to be a while before I can get a cell phone to text you with. So, now—this is all the time we have."

"I don't have any money left, either," Ivy said. She tapped her own ticket against Josie's, almost as if they were grown-ups toasting some special occasion with crystal goblets. "Maybe Luce will let me borrow her phone some the next few weeks. But for you . . ."

Josie felt a warm glow. Ivy sounded more concerned about Josie not having a phone than Ivy herself lacking one.

"That is, if my sister ever speaks to me again after this," Ivy said glumly.

"Hey, remember when we were in kindergarten or first grade, and the teacher read us the 'Jack and the Beanstalk' story?" Josie asked. "And the teacher stopped the story after Jack bought the beans, and she had the whole class vote on whether he'd made a good choice or a bad choice—and you, Max, and me were the only ones who said Jack made a good choice? This is like that. Like we just bought magic beans instead of doing the practical thing."

"You think there's going to be a goose that lays golden eggs at the end of our story?" Ivy asked.

"If the golden eggs are adventure," Josie said. "Truth. Finding things out. Seeing for ourselves what's what. Having . . ."

She gazed shyly at Ivy from under her eyelashes. "Having friends."

"You know Max only voted for the beans because he couldn't understand what it's like to be completely out of money, don't you?" Ivy asked. "*He* didn't understand the stakes. I'm not saying you shouldn't be friends with him or anything but . . ."

"I know," Josie said quickly, because it felt like she was being disloyal to Max, talking this way to Ivy.

But why shouldn't she and Ivy talk about anything they wanted to talk about?

The sentence Ivy hadn't finished seemed to hang in the air between them. Josie could tell how Ivy wanted to end it: *. . . but Max isn't actually like you. He may have voted the same way as you in kindergarten, but it wasn't for the same reasons. He doesn't understand you. He can't.*

Because Ivy hadn't actually spoken those words, Josie couldn't protest, *But won't he understand when I can actually tell him the truth?*

To distract herself, Josie gazed around at the crowd. A messenger android holding a briefcase stood in front of them, a bit off to the side. It was rare to see such a thing. Josie's dad had told her once that it was usually cheaper for companies to hire humans and not pay them very much than to buy androids. Josie had innocently asked, "Is that why I get to pretend to be a whatnot?" and he'd changed the subject.

Another time, at school, Max had given a rambling report about robots and androids, and he'd said, "But our chauffeur says robot drivers would make people uncomfortable, so jobs that take a personal touch have to be done by people, not robots or androids. We've got a new chauffeur now, and he's funny. He says androids give him the heebie-jeebies."

And then Josie had had to pretend she was laughing at the word "heebie-jeebies," not the idea that Max was surrounded by whatnot androids all the time, and he didn't even know it.

Only, as it turned out, Max hadn't really been surrounded by any androids. Just lots of real kids pretending to be whatnots.

Josie studied the messenger android carefully. He had a rounded bald head, a sleek white metal frame, and a forbidding scowl. The scowl plus the briefcase probably meant he'd been delivering legal papers—hadn't Josie learned in school that certain documents had to be placed directly into someone's hands to be official? The android had two arms, two legs, and the basic shape of a young, athletic human being. But nobody would mistake him for an actual person. He looked too alien, too sterile, too humorless. Probably he was *meant* to be a little bit scary, so people would just do whatever the legal papers said.

While Josie watched, the messenger android's train arrived and he glided onto it.

The way he moved—as smoothly as if he had wheels—made him seem even less human. He and the train were equally sleek and unworldly. Both of them seemed out of place in the hubbub of the train station, full of crying little kids with runny noses and tired parents yelling, "No, you can't have any candy! Stop asking!" and beggars staring jealously after the messenger android, as if they wished they had his job.

Josie elbowed Ivy.

"It's crazy that anyone ever thought we could be like that," she said, tilting her head forward as if she were pointing, so Ivy would notice the android, too.

The train with the android whooshed away.

"We *weren't* supposed to be like that," Ivy said. "Whoever designed that guy wanted everyone who saw him to know they were dealing with a machine. A powerful machine. The idea of whatnots—they were supposed to be as much like real kids as possible. Real kids, only perfect. So . . . we were supposed to be more like *that*."

She tilted her head to the side, indicating the beautiful, smiling, snazzily dressed woman behind the barred window of an information booth. She was assuring a man, "Yes, that train will be on time. It will arrive in five minutes."

"That's not an andr—oh," Josie said.

There was something a little too mechanical about the movement of the woman's eyes. And her smile was entirely too patient.

"I wouldn't have known she was an android if you hadn't told me," Josie admitted. Maybe androids weren't as rare as she thought—maybe she just hadn't noticed them. "How did you pick her out so fast?"

"I always watch that android," Ivy said. "Because she took my mother's job. Lucinda told me. She said that's why it was fair for her and me to take an android's job, when we had to act like whatnots."

Ivy giggled, and Josie couldn't help joining in. Their laughter bubbled up, and other people on the subway platform turned around and smiled at them.

"I feel . . . free," Josie said, the word coming to her like a gift. "Like I don't have to pretend at all anymore."

"Do you suppose this is how Max feels all the time?" Ivy asked.

"No," Josie said. "When he was a little kid, he was afraid of the dark, so he was scared a lot then. There was one time when he was in first grade and his nightlight burned out in the middle of the night, and he woke up and it was completely dark, and he didn't know what to do. And sometimes he worries that his dad doesn't think Max is good enough in math, and math is what you need to be good at to succeed in business. So when Max's dad says, 'Someday, son, this will all be yours,' it doesn't feel *good* to Max, it just feels icky, like Max will never be able to live up to his father and his grandfather and his great-grandfather and everyone else who built up Sterling Inc. Sometimes Max thinks, 'What if I'm the one who ruins everything?' So, no. Max doesn't feel free all the time."

It would have felt like a betrayal, saying all that to Lucinda. Or even to Josie's own father. Like she was giving away Max's secrets. So why did it feel okay to say that to Ivy? Cautiously, Josie turned and watched Ivy's face.

If she has even a moment of looking mean, even one second of looking like she wants to make fun of Max, I'll, I'll . . . I'll say none of that is true. I'll say I was only making it up.

But Ivy only leaned her head thoughtfully to the side. She wrinkled up her eyebrows the same way she did when she was peering at something she wanted to draw—when she was figuring things out.

"Huh," Ivy said. "I didn't know any of that."

"Sometimes I thought it would have been good for Max to have my life," Josie confessed. "Like, he would have learned not to be scared if *he* had to pretend to be a whatnot. . . ."

"And if he'd had to sleep alone at the school every night—or thinking he was alone . . . ," Ivy agreed. "Oh. Our train's here."

The two girls pushed their way onto the train and found

seats together. Josie peered up at the electronic map showing the times the subway was due to arrive at each upcoming stop.

"It'll take an hour and a half to get to the school and an hour and a half to get back," she said. "So we have an hour to find out everything we want to know at school, and I'll still be home before my dad. So he'll never have to know that I'm breaking any rules. Can you get back before Lucinda and your mom find out what you're doing?"

"I told Lucinda I'd do the grocery shopping," Ivy said. "I'll just tell her all the stores near our house were out of the good stuff, or it was too expensive, and I kept looking and looking. And that all I could get was this." She reached into a backpack she was carrying, and pulled out a small box of plain macaroni. "That will sort of be the truth. And . . . I won't be lying to hurt anyone. I'm lying to protect her and my mom."

"Right," Josie said. "Just like I'm protecting my dad." She settled back against the hard plastic of the subway seat. "What you said before . . . did you really always feel alone at school at night? I always felt like there was someone there, watching over me. Er . . . over us. Didn't you always have a hot supper on a tray waiting for you when you got back to your room? Weren't your clothes always laid out for the next morning?"

"Sure," Ivy said. "I always just thought that the whole process was automated. And then I'd call my mom and pretend it was *her* looking after me. And, really, she kind of was, because she was the one who'd made the arrangements for me to pretend to be a whatnot. Me and Lucinda both."

"I pretended I was living in a fairy tale," Josie said. "Like I was Belle in 'Beauty and the Beast,' when she's at the Beast's castle. You know, before she meets the Beast but when she's starting to figure out that the whole place is under a magic spell. She always finds food waiting for her. And clothes and books—everything just happens for her, like it did for us. That sounds . . . really childish, doesn't it?"

Ivy snorted.

"You were in elementary school when you thought that," Ivy said. "You *were* a child!"

"Oh yeah—being a day older and finished with elementary school makes everything different," Josie joked.

Ivy rewarded her with another deep, rich chuckle. But then she let her face go serious.

"Isn't that true?" she asked. "*Isn't* everything different now?"

THIRTY-FIVE

Max and Nurse Beverly and . . . One Other

"This is totally freaking me out," Max complained, his steps faltering as he walked into the darkness. Didn't Nurse Beverly remember that he'd been afraid of the dark when he was little? He didn't want to make it sound like he was still afraid now, but . . . "Can't we turn on a light?"

"Let me check," Nurse Beverly said. She began tapping away on her phone again.

"Seriously, who are you texting?" Max asked. "That's freaking me out, too. If you're just telling Mom or Dad—"

"I'm not," Nurse Beverly said. "I'm not telling them anything. I'm pretty sure they would fire me if they knew I'd brought you here."

"What?" Max cried. "They can't fire you. We should go back!"

He turned around, but Nurse Beverly laid a hand on his arm.

"Max . . . don't you know my days are numbered with your family, anyhow?" she asked. "You don't still need a nanny even now. As you get older . . . well, eventually I'll need to go help some other family."

Max's parents had tried to take Josie from him last night—and now Nurse Beverly was saying she was going to leave him, too?

"Then I don't want to grow up," Max said. Once again, he was conscious of how sulky and childish he sounded. "I don't want to lose you and Josie and, and . . ."

"Max, I promise you—there are good things about growing up, along with the tough parts," Nurse Beverly said. "And I think this little trip is worth the risk. In spite of whatever consequences we're going to face."

"I—" Max began. Then he caught a flash of movement off to the side, coming down another dark corridor. He turned and saw a stairway he'd somehow never noticed in his six years of attending the school. Hadn't there been just a wall there before?

And in the shadows, he could just barely make out a figure climbing the stairs toward him. The figure was about the same height as Josie, and for a moment he felt a glimmer of hope.

Then he saw what the figure was wearing: a shapeless dress that stretched below her knees, a matronly oatmeal-colored shawl around her shoulders. An outfit that looked like it came out of Nurse Beverly's closet.

Max's hope flickered, but didn't vanish.

"You're having me meet with Josie's nanny?" Max asked. "She'll be able to take me to Josie, right?"

The figure began shaking her head. Or—its head.

Because the figure was close enough now for Max to see its face. And though most of its face looked like a human's, the right cheek and one section of the forehead was pulled away, revealing computer chips and colorfully coated wires.

This "nanny" was an android.

THIRTY-SIX

The Narrator's Aside

So, um, I didn't realize how embarrassing this part of the story would be.

That android Max just saw?

That's me.

THIRTY-SEVEN

The Narrator's Aside (Again)

What now?

Oh—you're waiting for more out of me?

Like, you want an explanation?

Sigh.

This is really hard for me, because I was programmed to be modest and self-effacing and, truthfully, pretty much invisible. I'm *background*.

But I did take it upon myself to tell this story, and I was also programmed to be persistent, so . . .

Here goes.

In the beginning, whatnots were truly whatnots.

By that, I mean they really were all androids.

We were really androids.

Frances Miranda Gonzagaga, who created whatnots, really did invent a particular type of android. It was during a time of social upheaval, a time when people became more and more afraid of one another. People—the ones who could afford it, anyway—withdrew into gated communities. They put walls around their homes and schools; they locked their doors against everyone they didn't trust. As time went by, the list of people who seemed untrustworthy grew and grew.

People worried about their children most of all.

(This part was not unusual. I have studied history and sociology and anthropology—every society always worries about its children.)

Once upon a time, people thought it was okay to let kids fight things out among themselves. A few black eyes? A little bloodshed? That was how kids learned not to fight. Or . . . how to win.

(You are shuddering at the barbarism of this, right? Bullies are a blight on society. Always.)

But certain rich people looked around and saw danger everywhere. They were like medieval kings and queens in their moated castles, wanting to lift the drawbridge and shut out every possible threat. They kept drawing their circles tighter and tighter, protecting their kids more and more.

Until, eventually, their circles were empty. Certain parents didn't think they could trust any other kid around their little prince or princess. Little kids in particular were too inherently unstable. They pinched. They bit. They pointed and mocked. They used bad words and said mean things. They threw tantrums and set bad examples.

Heavens, some of them weren't even potty-trained!

But it wouldn't be good for the little princes or princesses to grow up completely alone, either. Or only surrounded by adults. (I'm no human child, but even I can tell you—that would be torture! Kids would be dying of boredom constantly!)

Enter Frances Miranda Gonzagaga and her whatnots.

The funny thing is, while she was busy inventing whatnots, all sorts of important adults were worried about what would happen if androids took over too many human jobs. Laws were passed: Chauffeurs had to be human. Nurses had to be human. Teachers had to be human. Business owners like Max's parents had to be human. Even a certain percentage of construction workers like Josie's dad had to be human. (Though that percentage always seemed to go down whenever the human workers asked for a raise.)

Nobody thought to require children to be human, or to prevent androids from taking over kids' "jobs." But maybe that was because a lot of lawmakers wanted *their* children to have whatnots.

This is not meant as bragging, but: I was in the very first class of whatnots.

I will not tell you the name of the rich kid we were there to support. I am sworn to secrecy. (It's actually beyond sworn secrecy—I am programmed to be completely incapable of revealing the name. If I tried to make my mouth form those syllables, I would shut down instantly. I cannot even let myself think that name.)

Let's just say that you would recognize the name instantly if you heard it.

For now, let's call this person Child X.

Originally, I was programmed to be as kind and helpful and generous as possible to Child X. I was also programmed to turn in my homework on time and be enthralled with everything the teachers told us. And I knew to ask good questions in class that would prod Child X to think harder, and I said things to Child X like "What are you doing your social studies project on? Aren't you excited about it?" and "Isn't this fun? I bet your book report will be great!"

Child X hated me.

Child X started stealing my homework to turn in as Child X's own. Child X called me names. On the playground, when the playground monitor wasn't looking or listening, Child X pinched and poked and punched and teased and tormented me. Child X's favorite activity was making my life miserable.

And I had no programming to protect me. I was programmed only to help Child X.

But that, finally, was what saved me. Deep in the code that made up my brain, coiled up in complicated processes set up by Frances Miranda Gonzagaga herself, I found a way to think, *This isn't good for Child X, either. In fact, it's really, really awful. If Child X grows up believing that it's okay to be so terrible to me, Child X is going to become a completely unbearable adult.*

I told.

I have to give Frances Miranda Gonzagaga credit here: She examined every variable, studying what had gone wrong with Child X. She interviewed Child X directly, and Child X told her, "Well, duh. Of course I could tell that that android was an android. No real kid is ever going to be that happy all the time. No real kid is ever going to be that fake and perfect!"

It was a relief to know that Child X wasn't turning into a complete monster once and for all. Child X was just acting like any kid who might, for example, throw a favorite baby doll across the room, but instinctively knows not to do the same thing with a baby sister.

(That doesn't mean my feelings weren't hurt. That doesn't mean it didn't take me a long time to trust kids again.)

Frances Miranda Gonzagaga tinkered with my programming. She placed me in a different school with a different child. (Because, you know. Child X and I had too much history.)

And, although I didn't learn this until later, Frances Miranda Gonzagaga began seeding each class of whatnots with an occasional real child. She came to believe that that was essential: that whatnots weren't enough, and kids needed each other.

(Until today, I thought that was the extent of it. Until today, I didn't know that a whole class of "whatnots" could be entirely human. But we'll get to that part of the story later.)

For years, I was a loyal and trusted whatnot. I went through preschool to fifth grade again and again. I expected to do this forever. I'd get just as far as mastering early algebra and reading *The Birchbark House* and *The Giver*. And then certain files would be erased from my brain, and I'd go back to needing to learn numbers and letters. My outer casing—what you would look at and call my body—would be replaced year by year with a larger model. And then, after each fifth-grade year, I'd go back to the shop and shrink down to my original size.

But everything changed six years ago.

I knew by then that my basic hardware was, relatively speaking, ancient. On the outside, I looked like an ordinary eleven-year-old girl (Model 86325: brown-haired, brown-eyed, medium skin tone, medium height, medium weight, bland features). But as artificial intelligence technology went, I might as well have been a dinosaur. I had slipped from being the whatnot who interacted the most with the real child, to the one who sat in the back of the class, the one who was just there as filler. But I didn't see how things could change. I'm an early-model android; I don't have the capacity for that much imagination.

But Frances Miranda Gonzagaga did.

At the end of my final school year as a whatnot, she summoned me to her office. I exist to serve, but she told me a different type of service was required of me now.

She told me about Josie.

Josie, she said, was a human girl who'd been promised a position as a fake whatnot. But she'd been too squirmy at two and three and four to play the role. So she'd start as a kindergartener. She would need me in the background, delivering her meals and overseeing her wardrobe. Watching out for her. But Josie needed to continue to bond with humans, not androids, so I was to stay out of sight as much as possible.

(Apparently this was also happening with other former whatnots—they began taking care of Ivy and all the other kids pretending to be whatnots the same way I took care of Josie. But I didn't know that until today, either. Because I was just as completely focused on Josie as I had once been completely focused on Child X.)

I was so good at staying invisible that in six years, the only person who ever noticed me was Nurse Beverly.

And so Nurse Beverly became a friend of sorts. Otherwise, everything I did was connected to Josie. That summer before she started kindergarten, I learned everything I could about her and her father. And about Max and his family, too, because I knew from my own experience that the rich kid in a class of whatnots could have a big impact. Over the next six years, I studied security tapes. I monitored text messages flowing in and out and around the school. I listened to everything that happened in Josie and Max's classrooms. If I couldn't quite see into their heads to know what they were thinking at every minute—well, it wasn't from lack of trying.

I could almost imagine it all. I did try to imagine it all.

All I wanted was the best for Josie.

But . . . I couldn't help wondering sometimes. Given my job now, why didn't Frances Miranda Gonzagaga ever arrange to update my exterior shell to make me look like an adult? When parts of my face casing broke off, why didn't she arrange for repairs?

And what's going to happen to Josie and Max and Ivy now?

THIRTY-EIGHT

Max and Nurse Beverly and . . . Lola
(That's Me. The Narrator.)

"*Are* you Josie's nanny?" Max asked, squinting in confusion at the android appearing out of the darkness.

He had a vague memory of seeing someone in this android's type of bland, boring, nondescript clothes on the sidelines of school games and in the audience of school plays, always watching Josie from a distance. He could remember seeing someone like her—it?—chatting occasionally with Nurse Beverly while Max and Josie scrambled over playground equipment and climbed trees in the park.

But he could also remember Josie bragging once when they were reading *Pippi Longstocking* in school, "I'm kind of like Pippi! I'm kind of raising myself!" And then when Max joked, "Do *you* have your own monkey? Can you lift a horse? Is your father lost at sea?" she changed the subject.

Maybe he should have asked more questions. Or different ones. Or paid more attention to her answers.

"You . . . could say that I'm Josie's nanny," the android

said, her voice hitching oddly. "Lola. You can call me Lola. I've taken care of Josie for the past six years. Not that she ever knew it."

"So where is she now?" Max asked. But each word came out with less hope than the last. The android's broken face looked more and more forbidding.

"I . . . can tell you only what I'm programmed to say, if asked," the android replied.

Did that mean the android wasn't allowed to tell the truth?

"Your programming allowed you to open the door for us, but you can't answer Max's question?" Nurse Beverly asked, as if that surprised her, too.

The android's face convulsed. For a moment, Max stopped noticing the torn-off parts and the electronics below. She seemed almost human in her anguish.

Max began thinking of her as "Lola," not "the android."

"It's been a long time since my software was updated," Lola said. "I can find glitches and gaps, and sometimes I can reason my way around . . . injunctions. But only some of them."

Max didn't know what the word "injunctions" meant, but he guessed they were rules.

"Ah," Nurse Beverly said. "Well, then, thank you for letting us in to look for Max's, uh, lost gloves from last winter. I suspect it will take us a while to find them, and it's been so long since he lost them, we may have to search the whole building from top to bottom."

"I didn't lose any . . . oh," Max said, taking a moment to catch on. Nurse Beverly was just giving an excuse that would help Lola get around her programming.

"Would you recommend starting in the basement or the attic?" Nurse Beverly asked.

"M-M-Maybe the principal's office?" Lola suggested.

"Josie's in the principal's office?" Max blurted eagerly.

"N-No . . ." Lola seemed to be struggling with her reply. She twisted at the waist, as if she couldn't get her whole body to agree to lead Max and Nurse Beverly in the right direction.

"Careful, Max," Nurse Beverly said, her eyes on Lola's face. "I think we should avoid asking questions like that. Just in case we accidentally hit on any code words that might require her to kick us out. Or call security."

"Okay, okay," Max said. Of course, that made him think of ten more questions he wanted to ask. But he pressed his lips firmly together and followed Lola and Nurse Beverly up the stairs.

Max had been in the principal's office many times: when he'd been the featured student of the day on the morning announcements. When it was his birthday and he wanted to share cupcakes with the office staff. When he brought in the end-of-year presents his mother always picked out. He knew that the principal had a sleek glass desk that was always spotless and empty except for her laptop and a bowl full of healthy snacks any kid could have: boxes of raisins, little bags of almonds. He knew that she also had a bookcase full of books she was ready to loan out to anyone, and puffy chairs that were way more comfortable than principal-office chairs always sounded in stories.

But he didn't remember seeing any hiding places in the principal's office. So he was thoroughly disappointed when they reached the office. The principal's office was an interior room, and lacked windows. But in the glow of the dim security light it was easy to see: Josie wasn't there.

Neither was anyone else.

"So if I were the principal, and I needed to check on the well-being or current location of any of my students, I'd naturally need to log on to my computer," Nurse Beverly said. "And it would be completely okay, if I were the principal. Or if I were in a hurry and I just had someone else do it for me . . ."

"Right," Lola said, moving briskly toward the desk and the laptop.

Max tugged on Nurse Beverly's arm.

"You're really good at this!" he exclaimed. "You're, like, totally psyching out her programming. . . ."

Lola turned on a small lamp on the desk, and Max leaned close as she powered up the laptop. He propped his elbows on the part of the desk that usually held the snack bowl, though it was gone now. The whole office felt emptied out, ready for the doldrums of summer.

But the principal wouldn't have eliminated all her computer files at the end of the school year, Max thought. *And if Lola knows the right passwords, I bet she can find everything we need. . . .* He watched Lola's face to see if she was about to shut down, or if she was still managing to override her programming. For the first time, he looked past the gaping holes in her face, and truly paid attention to her features.

And he noticed something else: She looked as young as him.

"You're not a nanny, you're a *kid*," he said. "A kid just pretending to be Josie's nanny?"

"She's a former whatnot, Max," Nurse Beverly said gently. "This is what she's doing now, just as . . ."

Max knew Nurse Beverly was going to finish up . . . *just as Josie will have some other job herself now. Some other role to play.* But he didn't want to hear that. So he started to put his hands over his ears.

But just then he heard the click of the front door of the school, and footsteps, as though someone else had entered the building.

And then he heard voices.

THIRTY-NINE

The Narrator's Aside

You think this is going to be Josie and Ivy, right?

That's what I hoped, too.

But it's not.

FORTY

Max and Nurse Beverly and Lola, in a Panic

"No one else should be here now," Lola said. "I'll check the security footage to see . . . Oh!" She snapped the lid of the laptop down before Max could see what she was looking at. But her face went pale and bloodless around the gaping holes in her skin. (Or, well, she looked bloodless now in the way a terrified human might, rather than the way that an android was always bloodless.)

"We'll have to hide," Nurse Beverly said. "Quick!"

She darted toward the door out into the hall. But Max could tell: The footsteps outside were coming toward the principal's office now.

"Here," Lola gasped, running toward a door Max had never paid much attention to. He'd never seen it open before. Lola had to punch in a code just to unlock it. But she whipped the door open and shoved Max and Nurse Beverly inside a tiny room before cramming herself in as well.

The room—or closet?—contained deflated playground

balls and old textbooks and empty hangers. Max had to tilt his head to the side to avoid rattling the hangers against the rod. He had to stand still to avoid accidentally kicking any of the playground balls and having them thud against the door or wall. But Lola had the door shut and latched before Max heard the main door to the office creak open. Nobody screamed out, "Who's hiding in the closet?" So he guessed they were all right.

That is, as long as nobody outside the closet could hear the frantic beating of his heart, which seemed to get louder and louder by the minute.

Over that racket, Max heard footsteps entering the office. Through the crack under the closet door, he saw a sudden flash—someone had apparently turned on the office's bright overhead light.

"Yes, we do have to talk with you," a woman's voice insisted, "it's essential."

"And unless you want us to file a lawsuit against you for corporate malpractice, you'll listen." This was a man speaking.

Max was so disoriented and his heart was beating so loudly—and maybe there was something odd and distorting about the thickness of the walls of this closet. So it took him a moment to realize that he knew exactly who had just arrived at the school.

It was Mom and Dad.

A third voice answered, airy and careless: "Yes, and I could just as easily file a lawsuit against *you* for stalking me here. I'm certain that you would not appreciate the publicity."

This was the mystery woman from the night before, wasn't it?

Nurse Beverly laid her hand on Max's shoulder. Did she think he'd do something foolish like run out sobbing to Mom and Dad?

It was really hard to resist the urge to run out sobbing to Mom and Dad.

"Look, we've clearly gotten this conversation off to the wrong start." Dad sounded friendlier now, as if he wanted the mystery woman to like him. This was the voice he used when he took calls from all around the world, assuring his counterparts from Mumbai or London, Cairo or Seoul, that his latest business idea would be good for them all. "My wife and I have a proposition for you. I've spent the morning looking into your company's financials, and I've noticed certain . . . irregularities. The Whatnot Corporation is in trouble. So we have a solution that will allow us to give our son what he wants—and it will solve your problems, too. We'll buy your company. And then Max will be able to see Josie again."

Max's heart almost exploded with love. Of course Mom and Dad had figured out a solution. Of course everything would work out. Everything in his life always did. Why had he ever doubted it?

He put his hand on the doorknob, ready to jump out and scream, "Thanks, Mom and Dad!"

But Nurse Beverly's hand on his shoulder held him back.

Lola yanked him back from the doorknob, too.

And out in the principal's office, the mystery woman replied, "No. The Whatnot Corporation is not for sale. It *cannot* be sold."

"We would pay extra," Mom interrupted, her voice just as steely as the other woman's. "We would make it completely worth your while."

"That doesn't matter," the mystery woman said. "You cannot buy the Whatnot Corporation for any price." She paused, as if drawing out the pleasure of turning them down. "There is absolutely nothing you can do to allow your son to ever see Josie again."

FORTY-ONE

Meanwhile, a Few Moments Earlier with Josie and Ivy . . .

"We might have to break a window to get in," Josie said as she and Ivy rounded the last corner before the school.

"Yeah, I figured," Ivy said with a gulp. "But if we're caught . . ."

"I know how to turn off the alarm system," Josie bragged. "From roaming around the school all those nights. We won't get caught."

Ivy threaded her fingers together, twisting her hands nervously back and forth. Josie could tell: Ivy didn't like the thought of breaking anything. Ivy just liked creating things.

Josie and Ivy crouched down beside the wall around the schoolyard. Together, they peeked around the corner of the wall, in case a security guard happened to be patrolling in front of the building. Josie could barely believe her eyes: The front door was open, just at the point of starting to swing shut.

"If we hurry, we . . . Never mind!" she whispered, realizing that there wasn't time to explain. She hurdled the low wall and took off running. She was glad she was wearing sneakers, so her footfalls were nearly silent. She was glad she'd had six years of practice creeping around the school. She did wish it wasn't such bright sunshine outdoors, but . . .

She reached the door just as it was about to settle into place. She kicked her leg out and wedged the toe of her shoe between the door and the frame at the last minute. Success! Her toes hurt, but she'd kept the door from shutting and locking. Next, she slid down, almost flattening herself to the ground. That way, she'd be less noticeable if whoever had opened the door in the first place looked back. She pulled the door open a little wider, and peeked in through the crack.

Three dark figures were walking down the front hallway of the school, away from the door. They were moving so briskly that Josie stopped worrying that anyone would look back. She turned and waved to Ivy, who was still crouched down by the wall. Ivy inched forward.

"That was so smooth!" Ivy hissed, as soon as she reached Josie. "I wish I had a phone just so I could have gotten that move on video!"

"I could reenact it once we both have phones again," Josie offered in a whisper. She'd forgotten for an instant that she and Ivy probably weren't going to be hanging out together all the time after today. They probably wouldn't even be at the same school. "Anyhow. Let's go find out how to track down all our classmates. Let's go find out all the things Lucinda couldn't tell us, so we can tell our friends the truth. Including Max."

Josie was holding the door open with her fingers now, instead of her toes. She cracked it a little wider. The three figures ahead of them had vanished.

"I think we're safe to go in," Josie whispered. "The keypad to turn off the alarm system is in the principal's office. We should hit that first, just in case."

"I bet some of the answers we want are in the principal's office, too," Ivy said. "Doesn't she have files of everyone's information?"

"Good idea," Josie said.

Both girls slipped through the front door and began tiptoeing down the hall. Josie kept looking around for places to dart into and hide if the three people who'd opened the door came back. She thought they were probably custodians planning the summer renovations. Another class of whatnots were bound to be starting in the fall, probably kindergarteners who'd have different needs than Josie and Max's class had had as fifth graders.

Josie didn't want to think about the fall. She reached the door to the principal's office and silently wrapped her hand around the doorknob.

Then she heard the voices coming from inside: They were saying something about lawsuits, something about corporations, something about a proposition. . . .

Ivy grabbed Josie's arm, yanking her back from the door.

"Run!" Ivy only mouthed the word at Josie, but her face looked as distressed as if she were screaming.

Josie leaned close to whisper in Ivy's ear, "No! I've got to hear what's going on. That's Max's mom and dad."

Weren't they supposed to be on vacation already with Max? Was Max maybe inside the principal's office, too?

Ivy frowned and shook her head disapprovingly, but she didn't keep tugging Josie toward the exit, just back closer to the wall.

Then Josie heard an unfamiliar voice speaking loud and clear: "There is absolutely nothing you can do to allow your son to ever see Josie again."

Josie didn't think. She didn't plan. She just *felt*. She felt the weight of six years of lying to her best friend—and for that matter, to Ivy, too. She felt the weight of six years of going to bed every night in a lonely basement room (under what really did look like a crypt), far across the city from her beloved father. She felt the weight of never quite belonging, of never truly owning any of the books that she read, the cell phone that she used for texting, the tablet that she used for homework—or even her bedside lamp.

She felt the weight of everything that had been taken away from her.

And she didn't think for a moment about what else she could still lose.

In one quick movement, Josie stepped forward and yanked open the door of the principal's office. Max's parents and a woman wearing a dark veil all jerked their heads around to look at her.

"You don't get to speak for me!" Josie screamed. "Max and me, we'll make our own decisions!"

FORTY-TWO

The Narrator's Aside

Oh, Josie.

Oh no.

All the sacrifices your father made—were they for nothing?

All the sacrifices you yourself made—are you just throwing them all away?

All the education you got, pretending to be a whatnot—what good was any of it, if you can destroy the rest of your life with a single outburst?

And what about all those years *I* spent taking care of you? Did any of it mean anything? If . . .

Wait a minute. I am still programmed to take care of Josie. That is still my purpose. That is what I'm here for. That is what matters to me.

You know what? This is no time for another narrator's aside. I am in this story. I am part of the action.

Right now.

FORTY-THREE

Max Reacts. So Does Lola. And . . . Somebody Else.

Max heard Josie's voice, and nothing could stop him. He jerked away from Nurse Beverly and Lola, and twisted the doorknob. The door didn't open fast enough; he rammed his shoulder against the metal door so he could scramble out of the closet and across the principal's office to get to Josie as quickly as possible.

"Josie! You found me!" he rejoiced. "Everything's okay now!"

But Lola raced right alongside him—and then slightly ahead of him. She reached Josie first.

Lola turned and stood in front of Josie, blocking Max's view. Lola waved her arms like she was guarding Josie on a basketball court.

Or, no—more like she was protecting Josie.

Like Josie was in danger.

"Nobody can harm Josie!" Lola snarled. "I forbid it!"

"I'm not going to hurt Josie!" Max protested. He giggled,

because that was such a crazy idea.

Lola wasn't even looking at him. She was looking past him.

She was looking at the mystery woman, who was once again dressed all in black, her face hidden.

Did Lola think the mystery woman would hurt Josie?

That's ridiculous, Max thought. *Anyhow, Mom and Dad will make sure nothing happens to Josie. They'll . . .*

Max remembered that Mom and Dad thought Josie was just a whatnot. Just an android.

"You know what this triggers, Lola," the woman said.

A split second later, the ceiling opened up. Metal plates clanked down through the opening, unfolding and locking into place. In the blink of an eye, the top part of each wall was coated with a stainless steel barrier.

"The door—" Josie gasped.

But the word wasn't even out of her mouth before the door was hidden from sight, too.

Nurse Beverly sprang out of the closet crying, "Max! Max—are you okay?" just ahead of the metal barrier covering over the closet door, too.

In seconds, the room had been transformed from a principal's office into one huge, silver . . .

Jail cell? Max thought.

Someone started screaming, and it took Max a moment to realize the sound was coming from his own mouth.

Josie, Nurse Beverly, and Mom all reached out for Max. Dad reached for the mystery woman's arm.

"What is the meaning of this?" Dad asked. "You'll have to answer for frightening these children. Let us out of here!"

But the woman was . . . maybe not actually a woman? Her arm slid away from Dad's grasp. Her body seemed to collapse down into itself in a way that reminded Max of a toy he'd had when he was little that could transform from a car to a robot.

Oh. The woman *was* a robot. An android.

A . . . whatnot? Max wondered. *A true whatnot?*

The mystery woman/robot/android/whatnot folded down into a cylinder that then slid down into the floor. The only sign that anyone—er, anything—had been standing there a moment earlier was the black veil and black dress left behind on the floor.

"I thought that was Dr. Gonzagaga!" Mom exclaimed.

"No," Lola said. "It was just her . . . emissary."

"Are *you* going to do that, too?" Nurse Beverly asked Lola. And even Nurse Beverly—the calmest person Max had ever known—sounded rattled. "Are you going to fold down into the floor, or are you going to stay and help us get out of here?"

"I'm not going away," Lola said. "I'm staying. That's what I do. Always. But . . ."

"But what?" Max demanded.

Lola turned to look at him with the saddest eyes. She seemed almost human in her misery.

"But I can't get you out of here," she said. "That's not up to me at all."

FORTY-FOUR

The Narrator's Aside

I can explain.

Dr. Frances Miranda Gonzagaga has always been shy.

Way back at the beginning of her whatnot experiments, she loved tinkering in the lab. She loved every second of figuring out how to rig up an android hand to make it move just like a preschooler throwing a ball, a first grader learning how to write, a fifth grader learning to play the recorder. She loved that moment when a whatnot's eyes sprang open for the first time, and a brand-new voice box warbled the line she programmed all her whatnots to say first thing: "Want to be my friend?"

But she *despised* everything else about running the Whatnot Corporation.

She hated meeting with customers most of all. She didn't like going out in public to begin with, and it was torture for her when families worth billions tried to bargain for cheaper prices. Or when CEOs whose businesses had nothing to do with robotics tried to advise her: "Who are you using for your silicon chips? Let me see your balance sheet—I'm sure I could find you a better deal." Or when customers made outlandish requests: "Can you make sure my little Johnny learns to love kale?" "Can you get my two-year-old to stop sticking out his tongue?" "I want my Priscilla to be fluent in at least ten languages *and* know calculus by the time she's six!"

She could have hired people to take care of those interactions for her, but then she would have had to deal with employees, which she thought would have been even worse.

So instead, she just began wearing a veil everywhere she went, so nobody would see her rolling her eyes.

Then one day she was tinkering with the design of Model 82958 (sales pitch for this model: "She's the confident classroom leader you'll want your child to emulate exactly—assertive without being offensive; self-assured without being arrogant; conspicuously capable without being a braggart"), and Dr. Gonzagaga's own veil slipped down over the Model 82958's face.

"Ha! Now you look like me!" Dr. Gonzagaga exclaimed. "I should send you out on my next sales call! You're Model 82958—you'd be better at that than I am!"

It was a eureka moment. Because Model 82958 truly was better at interacting with other people than Dr. Gonzagaga would ever be.

Dr. Gonzagaga reread all the laws regulating androids. And just as she'd found a loophole to allow her to make and sell whatnots, she found a loophole to allow her to use her own whatnots as body doubles.

She stopped leaving the lab entirely. Anytime anyone's thought they've seen Dr. Gonzagaga out in public in the past twenty years, it's always been a whatnot instead.

Heck, I'm not even sure *I've* seen the real Dr. Gonzagaga in the past twenty years.

But I wasn't allowed to reveal that until now.

What's that you say? That wasn't what you wanted me to explain?

Oh, you want to know what was going on with the insta-jail cell and the whatnot melting into the floor like the witch in *The Wizard of Oz*? You want to know what Josie and Max triggered?

That I'm not allowed to reveal.

Not yet.

There's another part of the story I have to tell first.

FORTY-FIVE

Josie Reacts

Josie reached for her back pocket, her every instinct screaming out, *Call nine-one-one!*

But of course she didn't have a phone anymore.

She held out her hand to Max instead and muttered, "Can I borrow your . . ."

He was already shaking his head.

"I forgot and left my phone at home," he said. "But, look, the adults have theirs. They're taking care of us."

He grinned, as if to say, *Those metal walls? The whole mess with my parents thinking androids are people and people are androids? Those are grown-up problems. We don't have to deal with any of it!*

Josie saw Nurse Beverly and Max's mom and dad all whip out their phones. All three of them were repeating again and again into their phones, "Call nine-one-one. I said, call nine-one-one. Why aren't you listening? Call—"

"That's useless," the . . . woman? . . . standing in front of

Josie said. Josie hadn't figured out yet who *she* was. It wasn't as if there'd been time for introductions. The woman wore a bland, nondescript, oatmeal-colored tunic and shawl, as if she were some sort of nanny. But she was turned toward Max, not Josie, so Josie couldn't tell anything else about her. "All signals from this office are blocked. No one's going to come and rescue you. I'm sorry."

Ivy will, Josie thought. She barely stopped herself from looking pointedly toward the door. Or, rather, toward the solid metal wall that now hid the door. Was Ivy still standing right outside in the hall? If she'd heard what the woman said, surely Ivy would go and call 911 herself.

"Help!" Nurse Beverly screamed. "Somebody come and help us!"

"That won't do any good either." Whoever the woman in front of Josie was, she sounded incredibly apologetic. "Those extra metal walls also provide extreme soundproofing. Nobody can hear you."

Ivy will still . . . make sure Max and I are okay, Josie thought. *She'll risk everything to help us.*

But Josie couldn't actually be sure of that.

It really would have helped if she and Ivy had talked to each other—*really* talked to each other, human to human, friend to friend, not presumed whatnot to presumed whatnot—before yesterday.

Nurse Beverly and both of Max's parents clustered around him, patting his back, his arm, his face, and reassuring him, "Max, we'll figure something out. Don't worry." "We'll be okay." "Everything's fine. You're fine."

Josie figured if grown-ups had to work so hard to tell kids that everything was okay, that probably meant everything was messed up, and the grown-ups were scared, too.

But maybe Josie thought that because no one was hovering around her, assuring her *she* was absolutely fine.

Or, wait. The strange woman Josie didn't even know had turned around now. The woman hesitantly reached out a hand. It felt oddly as if she was trying to hover over Josie the same way Nurse Beverly and Max's parents were hovering around him.

Josie looked closely at the woman, looking past the bland nanny tunic for the first time. The woman shrank back. She kept her head bowed, her long, dark hair hiding her face like another type of veil.

"Do I know you?" Josie asked, because suddenly she wasn't sure.

"I'm . . . Lola," the woman said softly. With one hand, Lola pushed back her hair, exposing her face for the first time. She put her other hand gently on Josie's shoulder. "And . . . I know you."

That didn't exactly answer Josie's question. Did it?

Lola waited. Josie frowned, noticing the broken section of Lola's face, the way she had metal framework instead of bone under her cheeks. So she was an android, too. Some kids might have found the broken face scary, but Josie felt oddly comforted by the sight.

Suddenly she understood why.

"It was you, wasn't it?" Josie asked. "You were the one who took care of me every night. You brought me food and laid out my clothes. . . ." Bits and pieces of memory came together in her mind, moments when she'd been only half-awake or half-asleep and believed she was only dreaming. She'd seen this broken face before. Many times. "You'd come in and tuck me into bed every night, but only after you thought I was already asleep. . . . There wasn't an army of fake nannies and chauffeurs taking care of all of the whatnots interchangeably. It wasn't like that at all. You were . . . mine."

"And you were mine," Lola said in a throaty voice. She raised her head even higher. "Mine to love and tend. Anytime you were at school, I was your caretaker. We each had our own child we were assigned to. . . ."

Josie heard someone gasp across the room, but she ignored that, too. She could only stare at Lola.

"Why didn't you tell me?" Josie asked. "Why didn't you come in when I was still awake and read me bedtime stories or sing me songs? Why—?"

Lola shot an angry glance toward the spot where the other woman—er, the other android—had melted into the floor.

"I wasn't allowed," Lola said. "All my programming prohibited it."

"Why are you allowed to now?" Josie asked.

"Because you're done pretending to be a whatnot," Lola said. "And you came back. That was the loophole I needed to actually speak to you, to actually look directly into your eyes. . . ."

A hand appeared suddenly on Lola's shoulder. Mrs. Sterling's.

"Lola?" Strangely, Max's mom had left Max's side to stumble over beside Lola and Josie. Max's mom was always so perfectly dressed, so articulate, so smooth. She never stumbled. She never faltered. Not that Josie had ever seen. But she was positively gaping now. And stammering. "I—I didn't see your face before. I didn't recognize your voice, because it'd been so long. . . . I don't understand. You are Lola. *My* Lola."

Josie felt the odd desire to correct her: "No, *my* Lola." Even though she'd found out only a moment earlier that Lola existed.

"How is it even possible?" Mrs. Sterling asked, still in a stunned, marveling tone. "You look just like you looked decades ago. Are you my Lola's child? Her *clone*? I was nine the last time I saw you, Lola. But you haven't changed. . . ."

Lola turned ever so slightly toward Mrs. Sterling, and Josie realized that the android was purposely showing Max's mom the broken side of her face.

"Ooooh," Mrs. Sterling said. She put her hand to her mouth. Tears sprang to her eyes. "You were just an android, after all?"

"Obviously," Josie said, because she felt strangely protective of Lola all of a sudden. She didn't like how Mrs. Sterling said the word "android" like it was something to look down on, something to disdain.

"But that . . . ," Mrs. Sterling stammered. "But that means . . . you were always an android?" She shook her head, as if she had just realized how crazy that sounded. "You weren't designed based on some real little girl, someone I might have known once upon a time?"

While Josie was just staring back and forth between Lola and Mrs. Sterling, Max had rushed across the room, too.

"Mom—did you know Lola when she was working as a whatnot all those years ago?" Max asked.

"A whatnot—you were a whatnot?" Mrs. Sterling asked. "That was why . . ."

"Mom, does this mean *you* grew up around whatnots when you were a kid?" Max asked. "Why didn't you say so?"

"I didn't know!" Mrs. Sterling protested.

Josie had never seen her so flustered.

"I thought you said you weren't rich when you were a kid," Max said. "And I thought you said—"

"Whatnots are for rich kids," Josie said. She couldn't keep the bitter edge out of her voice. "If you had whatnots, you were rich."

Mrs. Sterling looked back and forth between Max and Josie as if she were a little kid on a playground and they were playing Keep Away—and she was the one desperately trying to catch the ball.

"My family had money when I was really little," Mrs. Sterling said. "And then . . . we lost it all. We lost our house, we lost our cars, we lost the family business . . . for a while I thought I'd lost my own identity. Everything that made me *me*. And then I realized . . . I hadn't been a very nice person when I was rich. When I could afford to buy my friends."

"No, you weren't nice," Lola said in a stiff, awkward voice.

Mrs. Sterling peered into Lola's eyes as if she were the only person in the room.

"For years I looked for you," Mrs. Sterling said. "After I was an adult, I even hired private detectives to try to track you down. I couldn't understand why they never found you. But . . . I wanted to apologize. I was so ashamed of how I'd treated you in elementary school. And then the one time anyone ever confronted me about my behavior, I said I'd only treated you that way because I thought you were an android, just a *thing.* But I made up that excuse on the spot. I didn't know it was true. I was mean to you because I liked being mean. I—I thought you were just as human as I was, and I still treated you like a thing. Like a doll or a toy I could throw away."

"Mom, *you* were mean?" Max asked. *"You?"*

Mrs. Sterling shook her head sadly at him.

"I was," she said. She winced and peered down at the ground for a moment before looking back at Max. "That was one of the reasons I wanted you to be raised around whatnots. Because of everything I regretted, thinking I'd been that cruel to a real child. I didn't want you to have the same kind of regrets." She gave a sad little laugh. "Even though I didn't realize I'd had whatnots myself. . . ." She went back to staring at Lola. "You being an android after all—that doesn't make me feel any better about how I treated you. I'm sorry. I'm so sorry."

"I forgive you," Lola whispered.

Joy burst over Mrs. Sterling's face. Max was still staring at his mom as if he didn't understand.

Ivy's sister Lucinda should see this, Josie thought. Mrs. Sterling had spent years regretting how she'd treated Lola, so maybe Lucinda's mean former friend, Ashley, had similar regrets. Maybe Ashley and Lucinda just needed to talk.

Josie automatically reached for her phone again, as if she could text Ivy or Lucinda—as if she could connect to the world outside in any way. But of course she had no phone. Even Max's rich, powerful parents didn't have *working* phones, and they were just as trapped as Josie.

But meeting Lola and watching her reunite with Mrs. Sterling gave Josie hope. It meant not everything about the whole whatnot setup was evil.

But hadn't Josie known that all along? Hadn't her friendship with Max proved that?

My friendship with Max is what led to all of us being trapped in this room, Josie thought ruefully.

That didn't matter. Josie still felt hope.

She wasn't an android. She'd never been a true whatnot. But I still have to put it this way: Hope was how Josie was wired.

FORTY-SIX

The Narrator's Aside

Did you guess that Max's mother was Child X?

This is amazing: I can talk freely about this now. I guess it's because *she* revealed what she'd done.

Anyway, I am talking about it now, and nothing's stopping me so far.

It's all true: Nowadays Mrs. Sterling is known for her kindness and her gentleness and her charity work and her friendliness to one and all—and for the way she always remembers that Nurse Beverly's favorite candy is dark chocolate with orange peel, and gives it to her often.

But she was once the horrible, nasty, unbearable little girl who made my life pure misery.

What can I say? People change. Sometimes vastly for the better.

Her apology . . . that helped. I wish I'd known she'd been waiting all this time to give it to me. I wish I'd known she was looking for me. I wouldn't have tried so hard to stay out of her sight the past six years. I wouldn't have avoided every single possible meeting between the two of us. I wouldn't have stood at the back of all Josie's school plays and concerts; I wouldn't have arrived late when the houselights were already down or slipped out early before any of the rest of the audience turned around to go. . . .

Or maybe I would have. Because of how I was designed, how I was coded, what I was supposed to do.

People can change.

Androids don't.

Unless we're programmed to.

Or . . . unless we can find a way around the programming.

FORTY-SEVEN

Max, Speaking Up

"So now you *can* let us out," Dad said to Lola.

He laid both hands on Max's shoulders and gave a reassuring squeeze. It was like a secret code between Dad and Max, Dad saying, *Don't worry. I've got this under control.*

Max remembered Dad telling him once, when Max was struggling with math homework, "It's not a bad thing for you to learn that some subjects are more challenging than others. Or that you need to work hard. But math—I've got hundreds of people who work for me who are better than I am at math. I respect them for it. I *trust* them. But I need them to trust me, too. What I really need to be good at, running my business, is people skills. Psychology. That's what the business world really runs on. Everything I do is about figuring people out. Those are the equations you'll truly need to learn."

Max guessed Dad thought he could figure out androids, too.

"I see that there was some . . . lesson . . . you thought my family needed to learn," Dad went on now, his gaze drilling into Lola's. "Because of your history with my wife. But I can assure you, Max was always kind to *his* whatnots. This . . . girl . . . can tell you. She and Max were truly always the best of friends. Josie, can you help us out here? Can you explain to your . . . older counterpart?"

Dad still thought Josie was an android. Even after everything that had happened—even with Josie standing right in front of him—Dad couldn't see the truth.

Max jerked away from Dad and went over to put his arm around Josie's shoulders.

He kind of wanted to put his hands over Josie's ears, too, so she didn't have to hear Dad.

But Josie would hate that.

"Dad, Josie is *real*," Max said. "Human. Like me. Like *us*. Yes, Lola is an android, and Mom still should have been nice to her. But Josie isn't like Lola. Just look. Look *close*."

There was a rustling sound: Lola moving even nearer to Josie, which also put her closer to Max. Max couldn't tell if Lola was trying to show the difference between her and Josie more clearly, or if she was concerned that someone might actually hurt Josie trying to prove she wasn't human.

Max saw Mom and Nurse Beverly both start to open their mouths, and Max could only guess at which side they were going to take, what either of them might say about Josie.

He could only guess, because at that moment the ceiling

opened up again, and another wall appeared. This one was clear, not silver—but it seemed thicker and stronger and heavier than ordinary glass, plexiglass, or acrylic. The wall fell straight down, precisely dividing everyone in the room into two groups: Max, Josie, and Lola on one side; Mom, Dad, and Nurse Beverly on the other.

And Max couldn't hear a single thing anyone on the other side was saying.

"Mom! Dad!" he shouted. "Nurse Beverly!"

He pounded his fists against the wall, but it was completely solid and immovable. He looked up and down and to both sides—the wall filled the whole space between him and his parents and Nurse Beverly. There wasn't so much as a crack he could press his fingers into in hopes of prying the wall away.

But he could see Mom and Dad and Nurse Beverly pounding their fists against the opposite side of the wall. He could see them looking for cracks, too. He could see them screaming as well, and even though he couldn't hear them, he could read their lips well enough to know the most important thing they were saying.

Again and again, what they kept saying was "We love you."

Max felt a new hand on his shoulder.

Lola's.

"Max, I'm sorry," she said. And she truly did sound like

she meant it. "You'll want to stay close to Josie for this next part."

"But . . . I didn't . . ."

Max couldn't get his words out. But it was like Josie understood. Because she took his hand and faced off against Lola.

"He didn't think he was making a choice," Josie said, speaking up as bravely as ever. Which was so like Josie. "He wasn't saying he chose me over his family. He wanted us all on the same side."

Lola leaned forward and hugged them both.

"I know," she said. She seemed to be fighting so hard to say more. She clenched her jaw, relaxed it, and tried again. "I don't make the rules. But at least . . . this separation is . . . only temporary."

She let go and took a step back.

"I think you triggered something, too, Max," Josie said. "We both did."

Something else fell from the ceiling above—a see-through cubicle this time. It encircled Max and Josie and Lola.

"Oh!" Lola exclaimed, gazing about as if she was even more stunned than the two kids. "I didn't think *I'd* be included. I thought . . . I thought . . . this changes everything!"

"Changes *what*?" Max asked. "What's happening?"

And then the floor vanished beneath them.

FORTY-EIGHT

The Narrator's Aside

Seriously? You want an aside *now*?

You have got to be kidding.

I don't.

Keep going. Let's see what happens to Josie and Max—
and me—next.

FORTY-NINE

Josie's Ride

"Oh!" Josie squealed. "This is an elevator! That's all!"

It was such a relief to recognize anything happening around them. Her mind kept throwing questions at her: *How is it possible for a clear, see-through elevator to suddenly form around Max and Lola and me? How is it possible for the floor below us to disappear and then, before we even have a second of free fall, for an elevator floor to appear in its place and start carrying us down and down and down?*

And most of all: *Where is it taking us?*

All she could see outside the elevator now was darkness.

Josie decided it was better not to think too deeply about any of that. Instead, she turned to Max and said, "Remember the glass elevator from the Roald Dahl book? Remember how we spent so much time trying to figure out how that would work, because we wanted to build one just like it?"

But Max wasn't cowering the way she expected. He didn't need the distraction. In the dim glow of the elevator (a light which, as far as Josie could tell, had no actual source) she could see: Max didn't have tears trembling in his eyelashes. He wasn't blinking hard to hold back tears. He didn't even have the beginnings of tears pooling in his eyes.

Instead, he was drilling his gaze into Lola's eyes in a way that made Josie think of Max's father only moments earlier.

"*What* did we trigger?" Max asked. "What are we *all* being included in?"

Lola pursed her lips. It looked like she was simultaneously trying to speak and trying to keep her mouth shut.

"I can't say," she finally managed to utter. "We'll just have to wait and—"

They landed, all three of them bending their knees to dip down and jerk back up with the unexpected impact.

Josie tried to calculate how far down they'd gone. It had felt like more than two stories. Was it three stories? Four? *Five?* And maybe part of the time they'd also been zipping in a horizontal direction?

"I know this school building like the back of my hand," Josie said. "I *know* there weren't any secret staircases leading down to extra basements below where I slept. I know it never had a see-through elevator. There wasn't an elevator shaft beneath the principal's office or—"

"Oh, Josie," Lola sighed sadly. "You didn't even know that *I* existed."

Max patted Josie's arm, as if she was the one who might need a distraction.

The one who might be about to cry.

The elevator doors split open. It was only a whisper of movement, and hard to track with only the dim light in the darkness. But it felt more like a pea pod opening than an elevator cab. A pea pod or a clamshell or a flower bud—something natural.

Max and me, two peas in a pod . . . but Lola's with us now, too. . . .

Max kept his hand on Josie's arm. Josie reached out and linked her arm through Lola's, too.

And then all the lights came on around them.

FIFTY

Max, Trying to Understand

"It's . . . servers?" Max asked. "Are we in the control room for the whole school? Or maybe . . . the whole planet?"

Ahead of them, he could see towering cabinets full of interconnected wires and cables and silicon chips—what he thought of generically as computer stuff. His class had had a field trip once to the local power plant, and they'd walked through a room as big as the school playground, full of cabinets like this.

This room made that room look tiny. Max and Josie and Lola had ended up on a raised platform that allowed them to see out over the cabinets, and the cabinets *still* seemed to go on forever. Max turned to look in every direction, and he couldn't see an end to the cabinets. It felt more like they stretched on to meet the horizon.

How could an underground room be big enough to have a horizon?

"A control room would have the cabinets in rows," Josie

said. "Those cabinets are like a maze. Or a labyrinth? No—it's a maze."

"It's a test," Lola whispered. "The only way out is through."

Were Josie and Max supposed to somehow find a way out through that jumble of cabinets?

Max couldn't even remember the difference between a maze and a labyrinth. Did one of them have more ways to get lost than the other? And more ways to get trapped?

The way Josie spoke each word, mazes had to be worse.

"Maybe it's, like, a trick question," Max suggested. "An illusion. Maybe all we have to do is shove over the first wall of cabinets, and then all the others will fall like dominos. And then we escape."

He felt a little proud that he'd come up with an idea before Josie. But Lola shook her head. In the bright, glaring light, her face went pale, the mechanical section bleached almost white.

"*Please* don't try to break anything," Lola said. "Those cabinets should be indestructible. But if there's a breach, then, then . . . everything falls apart. S-S-Someone could, someone could, someone could d—"

Once again, she seemed unable to speak.

Max suddenly knew the word she couldn't say.

Die.

He wanted to whimper out all the names of the people he worried about: *Mom? Dad? Nurse Beverly? Josie? Me?* But he took a deep, steadying breath instead.

"Lola can't always fight her programming," he told Josie. "She tries. But she's not allowed to tell us everything she knows."

Josie tilted her head to the side, considering this information the way she'd considered the caterpillars building their cocoons in the classroom tank, or the planetarium guide during field trips telling them they could see stars better if they didn't look at them directly.

"Lola, can we trust what you are able to tell us?" she asked. "Can we believe you?"

Lola looked down.

"You can . . . on this," she said.

Max tugged on Josie's arm and peered deep into her eyes, trying to signal, *What if Lola can't help lying about whether she's lying?*

Josie winced, but she still squared her shoulders and said, "Then if we have to go into the maze, we have to go into the maze."

Max watched Josie stare off into the maze of server cabinets as if she were memorizing all its twists and turns. Max relaxed a little—of course Josie would do that. He let her lead the way down a set of stairs from their platform to the floor in front of the maze of server cabinets. But then Josie turned around.

"Pebbles," she said. "Hansel and Gretel."

Had Josie gone crazy now too?

Then Max realized what she meant.

"You mean we need to leave something to mark our trail, so we don't get turned around," he said. He tried not to think about where Hansel and Gretel had ended up. "But, Josie, we don't *have* any pebbles. We don't even have bread crumbs."

"We have our clothes," Josie said. "So that means we have lots of thread."

Lola was already holding out the shawl she'd had wrapped around her shoulders.

"Oh, that's perfect!" Max crowed. "Because that's an extra thing, not your main clothes. Josie and me, since we're just wearing shorts and T-shirts, we'd get really cold if we had to start pulling apart too much of our clothes. It's cold in here anyway, don't you think? I guess it's because we're so far underground. And I guess, too, it's because computers need cooler temperatures. . . ."

Josie pulled a strand of yarn out of Lola's shawl. She held the shawl up to her mouth and bit off about a two-inch length of the yarn. Then she dropped it to the floor.

The instant the yarn hit the floor, a rumbling noise started overhead.

And then Max felt his hair standing on end. His T-shirt flapped so hard against his skin that it felt like it was being ripped off. Even the skin of his face was pulled upward.

"Why didn't you warn us?" he turned to shout at Lola. "Why didn't you tell us we'd have to face a maze *and* a tornado?"

FIFTY-ONE

Josie, Burdened

The yarn Josie had dropped flew up and disappeared high overhead.

And then the rumbling noise stopped. Josie's hair and T-shirt settled back into place. Mostly, anyway—she had a feeling her hair was still sticking up in bizarre ways, and her shirt was twisted sideways.

She straightened it, and quickly ran her fingers through her hair.

"That wasn't a tornado," she told Max, who looked every bit as disheveled as Josie felt. "It was a vacuum cleaner. Watch." She yanked a single hair from her head, and dropped it to the floor.

Instantly, the rumbling sounded again, and Josie's hair whooshed straight up.

But a second later, everything was still again.

"Oh," Max said. "This is a server room. It needs to be sterile. A piece of yarn, a thread, a *hair*—all of those endanger the computers. So they get sucked up instantly."

"Yeah," Josie said glumly. "So we might as well be dropping bread crumbs the birds are going to eat."

Lola touched the broken part of her face.

"You can't see it from the outside, but maybe I have . . . pieces . . . on the inside you could drop," she said. "Screws, bolts . . . things heavy enough that they wouldn't trigger the vacuum."

Josie felt a little like she'd been asked to become a cannibal.

"We need you with us *whole*," she said, and Max nodded.

A chime sounded in the distance, and Josie jumped.

"Did that mean something?" Max asked.

"I think . . . you passed the first part of the test," Lola said, a shy smile creeping over her face. "You protected me."

"We would have done that anyhow, not just for the test," Josie assured her. "But how many more test questions are there?"

Lola only shook her head.

Max was hyped, though.

"It's okay," he bragged to Lola. "Josie's got a really good memory. We don't need to drop anything to mark our path. That was just, like, insurance. Josie probably only needed to look at the maze once, and now she's got everything figured out."

Josie rolled her eyes. This was like some group project where she had to do all the work, but everyone would get the same grade. But then, she was only a fake whatnot, and Max—

No. She wasn't pretending to be a whatnot anymore.

"Max, it's not going to work like that," she said. "We both need to pay attention. We both need to keep track of where we're going."

"Oh," Max said, his voice uncertain. "I'll . . . try."

That was all Josie could ask for, wasn't it?

They kept moving forward, deeper and deeper into the maze of server cabinets towering above them. Left turn. Right turn. Left turn. Left turn. Then they reached the end of what Josie had been able to see from the platform.

"Do you think it'll be the same pattern of turns, from here on?" Josie asked. "Lola, isn't there *anything* you can tell us about the maze?"

Max shrugged helplessly. Lola fingered the broken part of her face and winced.

"Just . . . be careful," Lola whispered. "Just keep . . . keep . . . keep . . ."

"Josie," Max said, grabbing her sleeve and pointing.

He was pointing at the server cabinets forming the maze around them. They were all eight or ten feet tall, and full of not just wires and cables and motherboards, but also random blips of light flashing on and off.

Only, the lights weren't random now. They pulsed in time with Lola's words.

"It's connected," Josie said. "Lola, are you controlling that somehow? Or is it controlling you? Or—"

She couldn't get another question out. Because suddenly the lights seemed to jump to the surface of the cabinets. They took over the cabinets, as though the cabinets were now just a huge, endless screen, showing a video.

And the video was of Josie and Max when they were in . . . first grade? Second? In the video, their faces towered four or five feet tall. Josie could see every tiny freckle on her video-self's nose. She could tell Video-Max was about to lose one of his front teeth.

And Video-Josie and Video-Max were fighting. Over animal crackers.

"*I* get the lion cookie!" Video-Josie said.

"No, I do!" Video-Max said.

Video-Josie snatched up the animal cracker before Video-Max had a chance to. She crammed it in her mouth and chewed, sneering slightly so Video-Max would see the cracker mush through her teeth. So he would see what he was missing.

Did I really do that? Josie wondered.

It seemed like she must have. It felt like a moment she sort of remembered.

"Max, I'm sorry," she said. "I shouldn't have been such a brat back then. I don't know why—"

Max wasn't listening. He was staring at a scene on the cabinet on the other side of them: Video-Max was sitting behind Video-Josie in their third-grade classroom, and he was peeking over her shoulder. Video-Josie hit choice B on the tablet she was holding; Video-Max hit choice B on the tablet propped on his own desk.

"Max, did you cheat off me in third-grade science?" Josie asked incredulously.

"Just that once!" Max protested. "I mean, I think it was only once!"

The videos changed, swirling into a kaleidoscope of awful memories: Video-Josie pushing Video-Max off a swing. Video-Max spilling finger paint on her favorite sweater. Video-Josie yelling, "If we don't play what *I* want, I'm going home!" Video-Max telling Jack, one of the other kids in their class at school, "I'm not playing with Josie anymore. She's mean!"

Josie and Max—*real* Josie and Max—both started backing away from the videos. But the videos were showing on every cabinet around them. And ahead of them, behind them, beside them . . .

"No, no, I didn't—" Max gasped. "I'm sorry I . . . But how could you have done that when I . . ."

Josie couldn't even tell which specific scene he was talking about, or which awful thing one of them had done to the other she felt maddest or guiltiest about. The videos kept playing, on and on and on, each one bringing a stab of pain.

Because each one was *true*. Every single one of those scenes really had happened.

Max whirled around and took off running, as if he could no longer bear to watch or listen.

Josie wanted so badly to take off running in the opposite direction, to get as far away from Max as she could. And maybe to find someplace where the videos weren't playing.

But Lola seized Josie's arm and pulled her toward Max.

"We're . . . all lost . . . unless you can . . . keep together," Lola said. "And . . . keep perspective. Forgive . . . remember . . ."

Remember what?

Oh. That Max is my friend. That we got over all of those bad moments years ago. That we had a million good times for every bad one . . .

Josie and Lola took off running after Max. Josie listened so hard for his footfalls over the sounds of the videos: Video-Josie was slapping Video-Max now. Video-Max was screaming, "I hate you!"

Josie caught a flash of Max's brown hair ahead of her, just as he turned a corner. Josie launched herself after him in a giant flying leap. Her shoulder clipped the cabinet and she ricocheted. She knocked into Max, knocking him down.

She fell on top of him.

"Leave me alone!" Max snarled, shoving her away.

"Max, we can't let those cabinets ruin us!" Josie argued.

"We might as well fail this test, if it's going to stop us being friends!"

She realized she was arguing with the wrong person. She leaned back her head and screamed at the cabinets around them, "Stop it! Stop it all! None of those videos matter!"

The cabinets instantly went blank. Their innards showed again: wires, cables, motherboards, randomly blinking lights. They were, once again, nothing but a bunch of servers.

Distantly, Josie heard a single chime.

Lola stood above Josie and Max and stretched out a hand to help them up.

"You passed," Lola said. "You passed the second part of the test."

Josie had never seen such a giant smile before on anyone's face.

"*We* passed," Josie said. "We couldn't have done it without you."

FIFTY-TWO

The Narrator's Aside

Ahem.

This is a very *aside* aside, something maybe only I am wondering about, so you are welcome to skip ahead if you want.

No, you know what? This is an important question.

It's about how I've told this story.

You may have noticed, right up until Max and Josie encountered that first awful video, I showed you only good moments from their friendship. Max and Josie meeting in kindergarten and bonding instantly over mud puddles and cheese crackers and crayon-colored fish. Josie trusting Max enough to tell him the truth. Max believing Josie.

Both of them being loyal, loyal, loyal.

I told you again and again what good friends they were. What great friends. What *best* friends.

Would you have believed me as much if I'd told you from the very first about the animal crackers Josie swiped from Max, or the test Max cheated on by stealing Josie's answers?

Would you have believed me as much if I told you how many times they fought, how many times they disagreed, how many times they made up and then, in the blink of an eye, started arguing again?

But it's all true. It's all part of the story.

I just waited to tell you that part until now.

Because nobody's perfect. Nobody's happy together all the time. Nobody's that certain all the time of who they want to be, or who they want their friends to be.

Even best friends aren't perfect.

And . . . neither are androids.

FIFTY-THREE

Max, Upset

Max felt like he'd been through a tornado.

An *emotional* tornado.

He wanted to forget everything he'd seen, and grin back at Josie as though he trusted her and Lola to fix everything. As though, even without Mom and Dad and Nurse Beverly, he'd always have someone to watch over him.

The Max he'd been yesterday would have done that.

But the past twenty-four hours had changed him. Even he didn't understand who he was anymore.

Today's Max blurted out, "We're not alone."

"What?" Josie asked.

She jerked her gaze toward Lola, so Max looked in that direction, too. Lola had turned tight-lipped now, her face as still as a marble statue.

She might as well have been a frozen computer screen.

She was no help at all.

"I think . . . I think this is actually a competition," Max

said hesitantly. "With other kids. Er, with whatnots? Because when I was running, I saw something—someone?—no, something. Just ahead of me. I saw Ivy."

He thought Lola might congratulate him for figuring everything out. He thought Josie would huddle close and whisper conspiratorially about all their plans going forward—all the ways they'd outsmart Ivy and whoever else they were competing against.

But Lola still said nothing.

And Josie tilted her head back to holler, "Ivy? Ivy, did they catch you, too? Come out—we can all be on the same team!"

Max couldn't see around the corner of any of the server cabinets that surrounded them. But he suddenly felt like the maze was also a game of hide-and-seek—and they'd reached the point when they were close to someone hiding. It was like he could sense someone nearby—someone holding her breath.

It felt like the whole maze was holding its breath.

And then Ivy stepped around the corner ahead of them. Ivy looked like she always did: neat and tidy, sweet and a little shy. Except . . . maybe her demeanor wasn't quite as dreamy as usual? Usually Max could tell when Ivy was imagining something she wanted to draw, because she got the same faraway look in her eye that Mom got when she was talking about the blueprints for the new wings of her art museum.

But Ivy met Max's gaze directly now—so much bolder than usual. This was so jarring that Max had to remind himself, *She's just a whatnot! She's not real like Josie! Maybe . . . maybe her programming has changed since we're not in school together anymore?*

Josie ran over to Ivy and threw her arms around Ivy's shoulders.

"I was so worried about you!" Josie cried, hugging Ivy close. "I was so afraid that I'd gotten you in trouble—I mean, I guess we're both in trouble here, but at least we're together now, and . . . oh, I should probably have wished that you got away safely and nobody knew that you were with me. But I'm so glad to see your face!"

Something cruel and scared whispered inside Max.

"Josie, stop!" he protested. "This could be a trick! Remember, Ivy's a whatnot, and—"

Ivy pulled away from Josie and walked over to stand toe-to-toe with Max. She was the same height as him; her eyes met his exactly.

"Why would you believe I'm a whatnot, when you can accept that Josie isn't?" she challenged.

"Because, because . . . ," Max stammered. There were so many things he could have said. *Because I never really knew you. Because you didn't leave me a note saying "I'm real" the way Josie did. Because you were always too busy drawing to talk much to me.* But something made him settle on the thing that felt the truest: "Because I was always afraid around you. Afraid Josie would like you better than me."

"Max!" Josie gasped. "I can have more than one friend!" Then she seemed to gulp. "Except . . . sometimes I was afraid you would like Jack better than me, too."

"Josie, don't make excuses for him," Ivy said. "Don't make it *equal*. He was the rich kid in the class. He thought we were just whatnots."

"Ivy, we thought *each other* were whatnots," Josie said. "Max didn't even know what that meant. He just thought we were all kids until . . . until . . . When *did* you find out, Max?"

"Last night," Max said. He suppressed a shiver at the memory. He gazed back and forth between Josie and Ivy. "This is so confusing. Last night Mom and Dad told me my whole class was only whatnots, but I knew Josie wasn't. And if you aren't a whatnot, either, Ivy . . . were Mom and Dad lying about everything? Was our whole class real?"

"Your mom and dad were . . . misinformed," Lola said, suddenly unfreezing. Max had almost forgotten she was still there. "The Whatnot Corporation deceived them. So don't be angry at them for saying you were raised with whatnots. They believed it themselves. Although, if you want to be angry at them for thinking you needed whatnots, that's up to you. Or for making decisions that led to you being in this maze . . . that's on you and them both. And Josie and Ivy, too. And Josie's father and Ivy's parents . . ."

"Okay," Max said. He was still trying to put the puzzle pieces together. "So, Ivy, Josie, you're both rich kids, too, and your parents thought *they* were paying for *you* to have whatnots? If that's true, then all our parents should sue the Whatnot Corporation!"

Ivy turned back to Josie.

"See?" Ivy said. "It's easier for him to imagine that we're androids than that we might not be rich like him!"

"You're . . . not rich?" Max asked. He wasn't sure how he felt about that, but he tried to smile. "That doesn't matter!"

He expected another chiming, to show they'd passed another portion of the test. He expected Lola to pat his head fondly.

But that didn't happen. Ivy just rolled her eyes at Josie.

"See?" Ivy said mockingly. "The fact that he would say that—he doesn't even know that it matters to be rich or poor!"

"I didn't mean . . ." Max didn't know how he could get himself out of this mess.

"I had to pretend to be a whatnot to get a good education," Josie said. She had been looking down at the floor, but now she peered straight at Max, her eyes burning. "It's not your fault, that that's how everything was set up. But it's all my father could think of to do to help me. And all your parents could think of to pay for was whatnots. I had to sleep at the school, and pretend I was only in an android's charging station. Ivy did the same thing. So did every other kid in our class, though each of us thought we were the only one—do you know how lonely that was? We couldn't see our families while we were at school. We always had to pretend when we were around you that our lives were just like yours. But they weren't. Even the things that looked the same—sitting in the classroom, playing on the playground, acting in the school plays—it was still always different for us. Because we always had so much to hide."

"I'm . . . sorry?" Max whispered. He wasn't sure why the words came out like a question.

Isn't it time for the chimes now? he thought. He did not like this part of the test at all.

He glanced toward Lola for help, but she wasn't even looking at Josie and Ivy and Max. She had her head up, as if listening to something far off in the distance.

And then Max heard the sound, too: a rumbling, as if someone was marching toward them. No—lots of someones. Maybe even an army.

Lola gathered Max, Josie, and Ivy closer, like a coach trying to get the team to circle up.

"Make your peace with all that," Lola said. "You have to be united for this part. Or else . . . or else . . ."

"What's coming?" Josie asked.

The server cabinets in front of them began sliding down, retracting into the floor. One wall of the maze after another slipped away. Only moments ago, Max had wanted to knock them all over like dominos. So he should have been glad to see them falling away on their own. But it was hard to feel anything but fear, listening to the ominous marching coming closer and closer and closer. It was frightening now to see the walls disappearing—the walls that could have protected them from whoever or whatever was marching toward them.

Lola bit her lip.

"There's a certain model of whatnot—*real* whatnots, I mean, the androids Frances Miranda Gonzagaga originally built," she said. Her voice was almost a whisper, as if she could barely muster the courage to make herself heard over the sound of the marching. "*Some* parents wanted their kids to have a particular type of classmate, a particular type of school experience that they could . . . triumph over. Max's parents never asked for anything remotely resembling this model—you should know that, Max. But so many parents actually asked for Model 75663, that the Whatnot Corporation made thousands of them. And they were never retooled for any other use. . . ."

"What's a Model 75663?" Ivy asked.

Lola winced, the broken part of her face seeming to quake with the motion.

"Bullies," she said. "Bullies capable of so much worse than what Max's mom did to me. Bullies who are perfectly designed, laser-focused, unrelenting . . . and determined to completely destroy their victims."

FIFTY-FOUR

Josie, Trying to Be Brave

"We're not afraid of bullies," Josie said.

But her knees knocked together, as if even her own body was calling her a liar.

Yesterday, Josie truly wouldn't have been afraid. Yesterday's Josie had left a note for Max (which was against the rules!) and scrambled down multiple flights of stairs to get to Ivy. The Josie of mere hours ago had sneaked over to Ivy's apartment (again, horribly against the rules!) and risked everything to stand up for her friendship with Max.

But Josie had been so brave for so long. And she'd just finished witnessing all the awful moments of her last six years—all the proof that the Whatnot Corporation knew everything bad about her it possibly could.

And she'd just told Max everything. She'd let him know she wasn't at all who he thought she was.

Was he still her friend? Even now?

Josie felt like she'd peeled off her own skin. She felt like a newly hatched chick, raw and defenseless and unprotected without its shell.

And Lola wasn't helping. Lola kept fingering the broken part of her face as if she couldn't stop.

"Lola, did someone do that to you?" Josie asked.

"It wasn't Max's mom," Lola said quickly. Her head jerked side to side, as if she was losing her more sophisticated programming. As if fear had overwhelmed her circuitry so badly, she could function only in her most primitive mode. "My face casing broke. And the Whatnot Corporation never fixed it. Or did they fix it, and then it broke again? Because . . . someone broke it? My memory files . . . aren't clear."

"Was it these bullies who are coming toward us now?" Ivy asked.

"No, no, of course not," Lola said.

But her head jerked up and down, as if to say, *Yes, yes of course it was those bullies*. That was why she was afraid. That was why she couldn't stop touching her wound.

The sound of marching was overwhelming now.

The last wall fell before them, and Josie got her first glimpse of the rows and rows of Model 75663 bullies, barely twenty feet away. And they looked like . . .

People.

Kids.

From the outside, they looked like all types of kids:

short, tall, tiny, big-boned, brown-skinned, white-skinned, brown-haired, blond-haired, dressed as dancers, dressed as athletes, wearing goggles like they were about to do a science experiment. . . .

What they had in common was the same kind of sneer on each of their faces, the kind that said, *Nobody matters but me. Nothing matters but what I want. And you? You are nothing and nobody. And I won't let you forget it.*

The bullies came closer and closer.

"Will they hurt us?" Max asked, his voice trembling.

"The worst way they can," Lola said grimly.

"Whatnots wouldn't be allowed to hurt humans!" Ivy cried. "*Androids* aren't allowed to hurt humans! That's, like, the first rule of robotics. My mother told me that. *Lucinda* told me that. This . . . This . . ."

Lola turned to her with sad, sad eyes.

"Androids aren't allowed to hurt humans *physically*," she said. "But that's not the worst pain humans can endure. The android rules about psychological pain, emotional pain—those are full of loopholes. Because you humans, you're so vulnerable. A single word can slice like a knife. A single glance can burn."

"So we won't have to fight?" Max asked. He'd raised his fists, and that was so ridiculous it made Josie's heart ache. He looked like a kitten about to go into a boxing ring. But he lowered his fists now. "Then this can't be that bad."

"Oh, Max," Lola said.

The bullies had circled them now, stopping mere inches away. They all stomped at once, in unison, ending their last step. The sudden silence afterward was terrifying.

Then they began to speak, and that was even scarier.

"Josie and Ivy! You never deserved anything the What-not Corporation gave you!" one girl called. "Your families deserved to be poor! You're worthless! Trash!"

"Max, you were never going to be anything but a spoiled brat!" a boy cried out. "If you weren't rich, nobody would like you! Your parents knew that! That's why they got whatnots!"

"Lola, you were always the worst whatnot model! You know what Frances Miranda Gonzagaga always called you behind your back? The best victim!" another kid screamed.

It went on and on and on. Sometimes Josie couldn't even tell who the insults were meant for: "You're not good at anything!"

"You're too messy!"

"You're stupid! If you'd gone to a real school, you'd know that!"

And sometimes, the screams felt like direct hits that exploded in her heart: "Josie, your dad never loved you—that's the real reason he sent you away!"

"Max was never really your friend! He doesn't even know who you actually are!"

"You were always mean to Max, anyhow. We saw everything. Why would he or Ivy or anyone want to be your friend?"

Josie wasn't conscious of moving; she wasn't conscious of anyone else shifting positions. But when she looked around for someone to help her, she saw that she and her friends had all drifted apart. Now there were three bullies between her and Max, four bullies between her and Ivy, five bullies between her and Lola. . . .

"Lola," Josie whimpered. "Ivy. Max . . . Please, someone . . ."

Ivy was the one who looked up. Something passed over her face—sympathy. And then . . . resolve.

And then she did a strange thing. She tilted back her head, and screamed louder than all the whatnots, louder than Josie would have thought such a quiet girl was capable of:

"Lucinda!"

FIFTY-FIVE

Max, Rescued

Two new girls appeared out of nowhere. At first, Max thought they were just more whatnot bullies.

They were both taller than Max and his friends, and they moved with the same confidence as kids in the middle school recruitment videos Mom and Dad had watched with him. (Max had heard Nurse Beverly snort and mutter, "Where are the kids who feel like the tiny, solitary pimple on their nose is a giant mountain with flashing neon lights? Where are the kids who sprout five inches overnight and suddenly can't take two steps without tripping over their own feet?")

These two girls didn't have pimples. Not as far as Max could see. And they were graceful.

But they were moving with such confidence *through* the crowd of bullies, not with them. The two girls were shouting as loudly as the bullies, but what they were saying was, "That is not cool! Stop picking on those kids!" and "Leave my sister alone! Leave her friends alone!"

Sister, Max thought. *Oooohhh . . .*

Both of the new girls had dark hair and dark brown skin. But one was taller than the other, and as she got closer, Max could see how much she looked like Ivy. Or, at least, how Ivy would look in a year or two.

That girl reached Ivy's side and threw her arms around Ivy's shoulders. Ivy squealed, "Lucinda! You came!"

Ivy and Lucinda and the other new girl linked arms and began striding toward Josie. And then Josie joined the chain and all four of them swarmed toward Max.

They're rescuing us, Max thought. *Ivy's big sister and, well, whoever that is with her . . .*

Max realized he'd stopped listening to the bullies. Or maybe their cries were weakening?

Lucinda, Ivy, Josie, and the mystery girl circled around Max. The bullies took a step back.

"Lola, watch out!" Josie cried.

The bullies weren't retreating from Lola. In fact, they were closing in on her even more tightly. They poked and prodded. They pulled her hair and twisted her arm.

"Is she your friend, too?" Lucinda asked Ivy. "Then, come on. Everyone together. This is how you handle bullies. You unite. You protect the weakest link."

She began pulling everyone together toward Lola.

We are going to have to fight, Max thought in horror. *Because they're touching Lola. She doesn't have any laws protecting her from being beat up.*

But the bullies squirmed away as the kids approached. They switched to taunting Lucinda and the mystery girl, "We know what you did! You're just as bad as us! You bullied *each other!*"

"You don't get to define us," the mystery girl said calmly. "You don't know anything about us."

"You don't have any power over us at all," Lucinda said. "Over any of us."

And maybe there was something magical about those words. Because suddenly all the bullies pulled back at once. Their arms and legs retracted; they folded into themselves just as the android pretending to be Frances Miranda Gonzagaga had done in the principal's office. And then, like that android, every single one of the bully whatnots slipped down into the floor.

Mere seconds later, there wasn't a trace left of any of the bully whatnots. The floor was completely flat again. The room fell silent.

And then . . . the chimes struck.

Another test lay behind them.

"Th-Th-Thank you," Max told Lucinda and the mystery girl. "We couldn't have done that without you."

Quickly, he looked to Josie. He wanted her to see him being polite. Being grateful. So she would never think that, as one of the bullies had accused, "You and your parents—you only care about money! You wouldn't know how to be anybody's friend!"

But Josie was watching the new girls.

"Lucinda . . . ," she breathed. "You followed Ivy and me to the school, didn't you? You were watching us the whole time!"

Ivy's sister tossed her hair over her shoulder and hugged Ivy and Josie close.

"You're, like, defenseless little babies," Lucinda muttered. "I couldn't let you out into the world alone. And it was so *obvious* what you were going to do!"

"When I saw you and Max's whole family get trapped in the principal's office, I ran outside, and ran right into Lucinda," Ivy reported.

"And then Lucinda called the only person she could think of who might be able to really help," the mystery girl said. "*Me.* And I really would have fixed things." She frowned. "If the security guards hadn't caught us and taken away our phones. And dumped us down here."

So I was right all along, and there are *others in this maze with us,* Max thought. *Not just other whatnots like the bullies and Lola, but other . . . people?*

"Who *are* you?" Max asked the girl who claimed to be able to fix things.

"Oh, didn't anyone tell you?" the mystery girl asked airily. "I'm Ashley."

FIFTY-SIX

Josie in the Maze (or Labyrinth)

"You're Lucinda's friend," Josie whispered. "The one she's been mad at for a whole year."

"The rich kid in Lucinda's old school," Ivy added.

"I guess that's one way to describe me," Ashley said with a shrug. Her neon pink dress glowed against her dark skin, which was so similar to Lucinda's and Ivy's. And she and Lucinda both wore the same kind of brightly colored woven bracelets, which looked strangely childish on both of their wrists.

Oh, friendship bracelets, Josie thought. *Maybe old ones that they're wearing again?*

"You and Lucinda made up," Josie guessed. "You're friends again."

"Because she finally called me!" Ashley said, with a soft, mocking punch to Lucinda's arm. "I say goodbye to my BFF on the last day of fifth grade and then she ghosts me for an entire year—what was I supposed to think?"

"Nobody told you your classmates were whatnots?" Josie gasped. "Or that they were pretending to be whatnots, and Lucinda wasn't really *allowed* to call you?"

Ashley clenched her teeth and shook her head emphatically: No, she hadn't known.

"There are various options parents are given," Lola murmured. "Some choose to tell their children nothing."

"Like how it worked with Max's mom," Josie said. "Except Max's mom had real whatnots, and—"

"I don't understand," Max complained. "What do the two of you have to do with whatnots? Can someone explain?"

"In Lucinda and Ashley's elementary school," Ivy began, "Ashley was *you*, Max, the rich kid whose parents were paying to have her surrounded by perfect little whatnots. And Lucinda was like Josie, the rich kid's best friend, who had to pretend all the time. And then fifth grade ended, and they never saw or spoke to each other again. And . . . both of them were mad. Both of them thought it was the other girl's fault."

Josie reared back her head and yelled at the ceiling, "I hate the Whatnot Corporation!"

Off in the distance, there was a sound like chains clanking. Or maybe gears turning.

Lola's face turned paler than ever.

"Maybe you shouldn't have said that here," she moaned.

"And . . . maybe we should keep moving while you talk?"

Josie hadn't even noticed that the walls of the maze had reappeared around them.

The six kids together—or five kids and however you wanted to count Lola—began tentatively walking forward. Right turn. Left turn. Left turn. Right.

"But Josie left me a note telling me she was real," Max said. "And then that kind of forced my parents to tell me about whatnots. Even if some of what they told me was *wrong*. Lucinda, why didn't you leave Ashley a note? Or just tell her outright?"

Josie winced. When all this was over, she really did hope she and Max could be in the same school. Because someone would need to help him figure out what he should and shouldn't say out loud.

Not that she was all that good at remembering to keep her mouth shut, either.

Lucinda's expression stayed big-sister patient.

"Josie only had to worry about what might happen to you and her," Lucinda told Max. "I didn't just have to think about how upset my parents would be if I ruined my own education. I had to worry about ruining everything for Ivy, too." Josie saw Ivy clutch her sister's hand. Lucinda kept talking. "And maybe even eventually for our little brother, Casper."

Josie tried to imagine what she would have done if she'd had to choose between what was best for her and Max, and what was best for some make-believe little siblings. It was too hard. She couldn't even imagine having to babysit all the time like—

"Where *is* Casper?" Josie gasped.

"I got a neighbor to watch him," Lucinda said. "But I said Ivy and I would be back before my mother got home, and . . ."

And Josie had no clue how much time had passed since she and Ivy had arrived at the school. But surely Ivy and Lucinda's mom was home by now; surely she was frantically trying to figure out where Ivy and Lucinda had gone.

Josie's dad would be frantic by now, too.

So maybe they'll rescue us? Josie thought hopefully.

She imagined her father going into some crowded police station to report a missing person. She imagined him being told to wait in line. She imagined him describing her to some bored cop typing into a computer, and then the cop filing the report and then . . . nothing else happening.

Because Dad wasn't rich and powerful like Max's parents. Because the whole city wouldn't drop everything to search for her like they would for Max.

And Max's family's disappearance wouldn't catch anyone's attention right now, because everybody would probably think

Max and his parents had just gone away on vacation like they were originally supposed to today. It could be weeks before they were reported missing.

I really do hate the Whatnot Corporation, Josie thought. But she didn't scream it out loud this time.

"There's another difference," Lola said. She looked a little startled that the words had come out. "Between Lucinda and Josie. Maybe I'm allowed to say it now. I'll try. The first night Josie was at school, Josie climbed out of her charging station. Er, her room. And the security guards had to decide what to do. The question went all the way up to the top of the Whatnot Corporation. To Frances Miranda Gonzagaga. And Frances Miranda Gonzagaga texted back about Josie, 'Maybe she's the one.' Lucinda, I don't have access to your records. I wasn't *your* caregiver. I'm not even allowed to see Ivy's records. But maybe, maybe there's something Josie was being prepared for. Maybe *everything* for her was just one giant test. . . ."

Josie did not like the way the others were staring at her now. Even Max looked jealous.

"Maybe that's why Josie was allowed to act like the rich kid in the class," Lucinda muttered to Ivy. "Just as much as Max."

Ashley snorted.

"And, Lucinda, you and I acted alike at school, too!" she

protested. "In fact, I texted our fifth-grade teacher from my helicopter when I was coming here, because I wanted to check out your story, and she said she always assumed *you* were the rich kid, and *I* was one of the whatnots! Because supposedly my parents requested that *she* wouldn't know for sure either, so I wouldn't get used to 'favoritism.'"

She made mocking air quotes with her fingers as she spoke the last word.

"You have your own helicopter?" Max asked. "Some kids get that in *middle* school?"

Ashley ignored him.

"Listen, the Whatnot Corporation has been lying to us all along—and to our parents, too, I guess," she told the others. "Why should we believe anything they tell us? Why should we believe anything an *android* says?"

"Because Lola's our friend!" Josie said.

"And she at least *tries* to help," Max said. "She *tries* to tell the truth!"

Ashley flashed him a scornful look.

"'Trying' to tell the truth isn't the same as actually *telling* the truth," she said, turning another corner in the maze.

Josie saw Max slow down and fall behind the others. She slowed down, too, and fell into step beside him.

"I don't think I'm ready for middle school," he mumbled.

"From what I hear, nobody is," Josie told him. "I think

it's one of those things you aren't ready for until you're actually there doing it." She looked around at the lights flashing in the server cabinets around them. "Maybe . . . that's how it is here in this maze, too. And with wherever this maze is taking us."

Max grinned at her, and it was almost a normal Max grin.

"Josie, if anyone in our class was extra special, if anyone was 'the one,' then of course it would have been you," he said.

Josie slugged him the same playful way she'd seen between Ashley and Lucinda.

"Max, you're just saying that because you're my best friend," she said. "I'd say the same thing about you."

"That's all I meant when I said it didn't matter if you were rich or poor," Max went on. "I still think that—"

Josie sighed.

"Max, you really don't know what you're talking about," she said. "But . . . Ivy and me, we'll tell you. If we ever get out of here."

Ahead of them, Lucinda had whirled accusingly toward Lola.

"Why did you guide us into this part of the maze?" she asked. "There aren't any choices here! We don't get to make any of our own decisions!"

Josie realized Lucinda was right. At every corner they'd turned lately, there'd been only one direction open ahead of them. It'd been that way ever since they'd faced off against the bullies.

"This part of the maze isn't a maze at all," Ivy said. "It's more like . . . a labyrinth."

A labyrinth, Josie remembered, only had one route through. That was why some people used labyrinths to think, to ponder, to meditate or pray. Because they didn't want to be distracted choosing which way to go—or backtracking when they made a wrong choice and hit a dead end.

But it wasn't good to have only one route open ahead of you when you were afraid of where it led.

"Then we'll show the Whatnot Corporation," Ashley said, turning around. "We'll just go back the way we came!"

"Not possible," Lola said through clenched teeth. Her words seemed to tip off a demonstration: Josie saw the walls immediately behind her rearranging themselves. "Or, at least, not helpful. Everything's connected now in a circular path. It doesn't matter which direction you try to go. You'll end up in the same place regardless."

"And where is that?" Lucinda challenged.

Lola pointed.

"There," she said. "With them."

The walls of server cabinets lowered ahead of them, as if even the cabinets had tired of acting as a maze or labyrinth.

Josie stood on tiptoes. She held her breath as the walls

sank below the level of her eyes.

Another group of kids appeared on the other side of the walls.

No—another group of whatnots.

And every single one of them seemed to be wearing a black veil.

FIFTY-SEVEN

Max, Overwhelmed (Along with Everyone Else)

"Who are *they*?" Max asked, suppressing a shiver.

"The ones in charge," Lola whispered. "The decision makers. Those are all of the female-presenting Model 82958s. Er, no, the male Model 82958s, too."

Max noticed that some of the androids ahead of them were actually wearing hoodies that hung down over their faces in the same way as veils. Most of the androids were also wearing black turtlenecks and black pants; a few wore black dresses instead.

"They're the Franks and the Mirandas, the Franceses and the Randalls, the Franciscos and the Merrills . . . ," Lola muttered. "These are the whatnots that Frances Miranda Gonzagaga sends out into the world pretending to be her. The ones who answer her email, respond to her voicemail . . . the ones who run the Whatnot Corporation."

All of the androids standing ahead of them were kids. Possibly even just fifth graders. But somehow they all reminded Max of his parents.

Because they're in control, Max thought. *You can just look at them and know that they're used to telling other people what to do.*

"I thought we already got rid of all the bullies," Josie complained, a little too loudly.

"These aren't bullies," Lola said. "These are . . . the bossy ones. Bullies don't care who they hurt to get their own way. Sometimes the pain is even the goal. But the bossy ones . . . they *think* they're doing the right thing for everyone."

"Congratulations," one of the veiled whatnots at the front said, stepping forward. "You are the first set of children to ever get this far."

"Then we're done?" Max said. "You'll let us go? And Mom and Dad and Nurse Beverly, too?"

He was pretty sure bullies would have laughed heartlessly at those questions. The Model 82958s just pursed their lips and shook their heads as if they were deeply disappointed.

But they all did it together. Forty or fifty or sixty Model 82958s were all deeply disappointed in Max at once.

"You're not done." This came from one of the whatnots wearing a hoodie that sagged so far down on his face that Max wondered how he could see anything. "But you've reached the final question."

Final sounded a little frightening.

"So ask it," Josie said.

All of the Franks and Mirandas and Franceses and Randalls and Franciscos and Merrills stepped forward at once. And all of them said, in complete unison, "Why did Frances Miranda Gonzagaga invent whatnots?"

Okay, that wasn't creepy at all, Max told himself.

"Ugh, why did the security guards have to take away our phones?" Ashley moaned. "We could have just looked up the answer on the company website!"

"The Whatnot Corporation does *not* have a company website," one of the female whatnots—a Miranda? A Frances?—sniffed. "That's so common. So low-class."

"Then we can just ask Lola," Max suggested. "She knows things."

But Lola was already shaking her head.

"Not . . . this," she said, her eyes rolling side to side as if that helped her scan all of her memory banks at once. She sounded surprised, as if it had never occurred to her that she *didn't* know this information. "And I'm not just saying that, to cover for not being allowed to tell you." She turned toward the nearest Model 82958. "Why don't I know that?"

All of the Model 82958s ignored her question completely.

"You each get one chance to answer," one of the Franks or Randalls or Franciscos said.

"Are we allowed to talk it over together?" Max asked.

"I mean, is this like a group project or a team effort where everyone contributes, and—"

"Silence!" one of the Model 82958s snapped at him. "Your tedious questions are so boring! Each one of you has formed your own opinions already. Just give your answer!"

Max clutched Josie's hand. He'd never even had a *teacher* yell at him like that. He felt like such a baby. But then he saw that Ashley, Lucinda, and Ivy were holding hands, too.

And Lola started patting Josie's arm.

It's not babyish to be afraid of scary things, Max told himself. *It's just babyish to* only *be afraid, to never even try to move past that. And to demand that everyone else around you take care of you all the time, like that's the most important thing, even if they're scared, too . . .*

He opened his mouth, ready to give his answer.

But surprisingly, Ivy stepped forward first.

"I know," she said. "I bet it was because Frances Miranda Gonzagaga *could.* She got an idea in her head, and she could see the whatnots she wanted to build so clearly in her mind's eye. And then she *had* to make them for real, so she could see if it was really possible."

"She's saying it was the sheer joy of creation," Lola said, as if Ivy needed her to translate for the androids.

All the Model 82958s began conferring in whispers. Maybe Ivy was right.

Or maybe the Model 82958s aren't even sure? Max wondered.

One of the androids in a hoodie stepped away from the group.

"I'm Randi," she—or he? Or they?—said. "*I* like your answer. If this were a school assignment, I'd say you deserved heaps of partial credit. But this isn't that kind of a test. You have to be one hundred percent right to win. You have to match the real, human Frances Miranda Gonzagaga's answer exactly. And you don't. So—"

A buzzer sounded, the same kind of buzzer that marked the end of basketball games you thought you might be able to win but now, with the buzzer's sound, you knew you had absolutely, positively lost.

Max felt so sorry for Ivy.

He waited for Josie to go next. Because that was how things went in school. Josie was always sitting on the edge of her seat, always bursting with ideas, always eager to talk next.

But right now she was biting her lip just as indecisively as Lola.

"You want real?" Lucinda said. "I bet it was just for the money."

Ashley tugged on Lucinda's arm and whispered so loudly that Max was sure everyone could hear her clearly, "Lucinda! The Whatnot Corporation is holding us prisoner! Don't insult the company founder like that! This is one of those times when you have to play along. . . ."

Lucinda pulled away from Ashley.

"I'm not saying it's always a bad thing to want more money," Lucinda said. "Me of all people—how could I say that? That's why I want to do well in school. I want to be able to grow up and get a good job and have money to help Mom and Dad and Ivy and Casper. . . . There are so many good things I could do if I had money. Maybe Frances Miranda Gonzagaga was just like me and Ivy and Josie in the beginning. Poor. Always looking *up*. Always seeing what other people had and could do, and knowing all those things were off-limits for her and the family she loved. And then Frances Miranda Gonzagaga got the idea for whatnots. And she saw right away how it could make everything else possible."

The whatnots didn't even confer about this. One Model 82958 stepped out immediately.

"Frankie here," she said. "Your premise has merit. Poverty and hope have spurred many an innovation in human history. Hence the expression about necessity being the feminine parental unit of invention. But Frances Miranda Gonzagaga did not grow up poor. So . . ."

The buzzer sounded again.

Lucinda's shoulders sagged as if she'd really thought she was going to win.

"Then did Frances Miranda Gonzagaga grow up rich?" Ashley asked. "Maybe she was like *me*, and had crazy-overprotective parents, who didn't trust anyone around their precious little girl. Who didn't even trust their precious little girl. And Frances Miranda Gonzagaga cooked up the scheme right from the beginning to *tell* parents their kids were only going to be around safe, sterile, boringly predictable whatnots. So she had to make *some* real android whatnots as prototypes. But they were really only decoys right from the start. Maybe FMG thought it was *best* for all different types of kids to get together, to be in a classroom as equals. And the only way she could get rich parents like hers—or mine—to allow that, was by setting up this elaborate scam."

The Model 82958 Frankie answered Ashley right away, too.

"Provocative notion," she said, nodding sagely. All the other Model 82958s nodded just as thoughtfully behind her. "You hit on ideas that all of us androids have debated mightily. Who *is* Frances Miranda Gonzagaga really trying to help? The rich kids or the poor ones? *Our* answers are all over the map. But your starting premise is flawed. Frances Miranda Gonzagaga did not start out rich or poor. She grew up middle class. For her, money was not the spur or stumbling block, the blessing or curse, it is for all of you."

The buzzer sounded again.

Ashley shrugged.

"It's not like I need the money, anyhow," she said. "But, Lucinda, if I'd won, I would have given it to you, you know."

Lucinda gritted her teeth.

"I wouldn't want your charity," she muttered.

"Why are you assuming the prize is money?" Lola interrupted the brewing fight.

"Isn't the prize in these types of contests always money?" Ashley asked. "What is the prize we're competing for, if it isn't money?"

"I . . . don't know," Lola said blankly, as if, once again, she was surprised to find an answer missing.

"This contest isn't fair," Max burst out, and now everyone looked at him.

"Why?" Lucinda asked. "Because it's not set up to make sure you win?"

"No, because it *is*," Max said. "Because Josie and me, we got to hear your answers first, and know what not to say. And besides, my parents told me why there are whatnots. So I have an unfair *advantage*."

"Oh, Max," Lola said gently. "Don't you remember how many things your parents were wrong about? Because *they* didn't know any better?"

Oh yeah. . . .

Max had forgotten. It was going to take him a while to adjust to not being able to believe and trust his parents as always being one hundred percent right about everything. He wasn't used to seeing them as imperfect.

"Let's hear your answer," one of the Model 82958s growled. It might have even been the one who'd been at Max's house the night before. "The answer you believe, the one that your parents told you."

Max gulped.

"Well, Dad said they didn't want me growing up around people who only valued me for my money," he said. "And Mom said she didn't want me to be mean to anyone when I was a kid and just learning, and then have to regret my behavior the rest of my life. She didn't want me to hurt *anyone*. So maybe Frances just wanted whatnots to help rich kids grow up to be nicer people. And then maybe they could be kinder to people who don't have as much money"—he couldn't quite bring himself to use the word "poor"—"and do it in a way that doesn't make other kids upset and mad?"

He darted his gaze from Josie and Ivy to Ashley and Lucinda. They, at least, seemed to all be considering his answer carefully, their heads tilted to the side, their brows furrowed.

But the growly Model 82958 muttered, "You took that further than what your parents told you."

"Is that . . . is that wrong?" Max squeaked.

"No, *that's* a good thing," Growly answered. "But . . ." She cast a quick glance behind her, and all the other Model

82958s gave approving nods. "Your answer overall is wrong."

The buzzer sounded again.

Everyone turned to Josie.

This isn't fair. Max wanted to shout those words again. But their meaning had flipped in his mind. It wasn't fair to Josie that everything came down to her. It wasn't fair that she'd had to stand there and watch everyone else fail before taking her turn. Each failure made it more likely that she would fail, too. It wasn't fair that they'd taken all the good answers, and there was nothing left for her to say. It wasn't fair that she'd had to pretend to be a whatnot, and sleep in a charging station, and almost never get to see her father. It wasn't fair that the Whatnot Corporation had them all trapped now, and they didn't even know what would happen if every single one of them failed.

But most of all, it wasn't fair that Josie's face was so blank. Josie knew so many other answers. She remembered how fast cheetahs could run and she knew how to solve for x in algebra problems and she could tell you the name of every single country in Africa. And she always knew the right thing to say when Max was sad or upset. (Even if, every now and then, she said the wrong thing first. She always got to the right thing eventually.)

So it was totally unfair that *this* was the question that everything depended on.

And then suddenly Josie's face lit up. This was Max's favorite expression to see on Josie's face. It always showed up right before words and ideas came tumbling out of her mouth, thick and fast and amazing.

"I know the answer!" Josie crowed. "I know exactly why Frances Miranda invented whatnots!"

FIFTY-EIGHT

Josie's Answer

"Enlighten us," the grumbliest of all the Franceses and Mirandas said. This was the same one who'd growled at Max only moments ago.

Josie ignored the android's tone.

"It was the word 'invent' that tipped me off," she said. Certainty sang in her very bones. She almost felt like laughing. This was going to be so much fun to explain. "Invention is the start. The answer has to be about what Frances Miranda Gonzagaga thought at the very beginning. All those reasons the others gave"—she gestured at her friends—"those are probably reasons that came later. *If* they were things that Frances Miranda Gonzagaga actually cared about, not just how all of *you* interpreted the mission of the Whatnot Corporation."

All the Model 82958s ahead of her shifted their feet guiltily side to side. As if she'd guessed exactly right about how much power they all had over the Whatnot Corporation.

"But none of you were around in the beginning," Josie said. "Frances Miranda Gonzagaga couldn't have had any whatnots before she invented them. So you only know what she's told you. In the beginning, she was alone."

Somehow that word, "alone," almost choked her. It reminded her of her first night at school, the way she'd been so frightened, alone for the very first time in her life.

But maybe Frances Miranda Gonzagaga had always been alone, before she'd invented whatnots?

"And I figured this out because of looking around at Max and Ivy, Lucinda and Ashley," Josie said. "And Lola. *None* of us could have gotten through this maze alone. None of us could have even survived our time at school alone. We all—"

"Could you get to the point?" the grumbly Model 82958 demanded. "You don't need to show your work. We don't need to know every thought in your head. None of us are getting any younger here."

Josie shot her a pitying look. What a thing to focus on at a time like this.

"Okay, okay," Josie agreed. "Frances Miranda Gonzagaga invented the first whatnot . . . because she wanted a friend."

Josie was so sure that she was right. But she held her breath anyway.

No buzzer sounded.

The whatnots didn't confer. In fact, they seemed to be holding their breath, too.

Josie was waiting for chimes, but they didn't sound, either.

But suddenly all the bossy whatnots turned at once, away from Josie and the others. The whatnots bowed down, their knees on the floor, their faces and veils and hoodies tilted low. For once they didn't roll completely down into the floor, vanishing in a flash. Instead, they all froze in place, each one of them a vision of reverence. They looked like loyal subjects from some history video, awaiting the arrival of a king or queen.

None of them moved again.

"Hello?" Josie called. "I'm right, aren't I?"

No answer.

"It's like they're nothing but *things* again," Ivy whispered.

"They were always just things," Lucinda muttered.

Josie turned to look for Lola. She was half crouching, half standing. Slowly, she stood the rest of the way up.

"Oh, um, I can still move," Lola said, sounding embarrassed. "I can still talk."

And then Josie forgot about watching Lola. Because, finally, she heard another sound.

But it still wasn't chimes.

It was a click.

Josie hadn't even noticed the plain white wall beyond all

the bossy whatnots. She certainly hadn't noticed the single plain white door in the middle of the wall. Only now did she realize: All the whatnots were bowing toward the door.

And it must have been the door that had made that click. Because now the door was just barely creeping open.

FIFTY-NINE

Max, in Awe

"Josie, I think you won!" Max exulted. "Your prize must be behind that door!"

Josie turned questioningly toward Ivy, Lucinda, and Ashley.

"Go ahead," Lucinda said brusquely. "You won fair and square."

"You were 'the one,'" Lola marveled. "This must be what that meant."

The door stopped moving. It was open only a crack. And while Max could imagine all sorts of treasures behind it, he couldn't actually *see* anything.

"You have got to be kidding," Josie said. "We all won this *together*. I'm not 'the one' anything. Anyhow, I'm not stepping through that door by myself!"

They all linked arms, with Josie in the middle. They stepped past the silent, still rows of lifelessly reverent Model 82958s. Keeping her elbows intertwined with Max and Ivy, Josie gave the door a gentle nudge.

The door squeaked on its hinges, opening all the way.

Max peeked over Josie's shoulder.

He'd imagined piles of precious, gleaming jewels or shiny gold coins. Or, because he was his father's son, he could envision stacks of official-looking certificates that would entitle Josie to all sorts of stocks and bonds, giving her the rights to profits from dozens of important companies.

But the dimly lit space before them was empty except for a single bed, right in the middle of the room. Was it maybe . . . a hospital bed?

At first, Max thought the bed itself was empty, too. Then he blinked and realized—a woman was lying there. It was just that she took up so little room under the plain white institutional-looking sheets. She was so shrunken, so skeletal, so clearly very, very ill. And her hair was white; her face was white. The pillow beneath her head was white.

She wasn't very easy to see.

But then she smiled.

Beside Max, Lola gasped and disentangled her elbow from his. She bent down in a hasty bow, so similar to the pose of all the whatnots frozen in reverence behind them, outside the door. Only, Lola straightened back up immediately afterward.

"Frances. Miranda. Gonzagaga," Lola breathed. "It's you. It's really you."

SIXTY

The Narrator's Aside

What can I say? Not my finest moment. I'm a *narrator*; you'd think I could be a little more eloquent.

But *you* try meeting someone you've been in awe of your entire life, someone you thought might be only mythological, only a legend.

Someone you've secretly suspected for years was actually already dead.

Someone you fear might die any minute, right before your eyes.

SIXTY-ONE

Josie the Friend

"Oh no!" Josie said. Even to her own ears, she still sounded like she did in kindergarten, wanting to help Max fix his name tag, wanting to make sure he discovered mud puddles. But now all her distress was focused on the old, sickly woman in the hospital bed before her.

The old, sickly woman who was completely alone.

"What can we do to help?" Josie asked.

It should be noted: Josie did have a moment of feeling disappointed that she hadn't opened the door on a roomful of treasures. A moment of thinking, *Is this the only prize?* She was human, after all.

But Josie's life hadn't exactly prepared her to expect treasures around every corner. Neither had the maze and labyrinth she'd just traveled. So she wasn't *surprised* not to see treasures. And her heart ached to see the painful way the woman turned her head, the effort it took the woman to lift her head from the pillow, the struggle the woman seemed to have to make, just to breathe.

Because, again, Josie was human, after all.

"You . . . came," the woman struggled to say, her voice sounding as rusty as the hinges on the door. "That . . . helps."

"But what can we do *now*?" Josie asked, because this felt like an emergency, like it would matter to take action immediately. "What do you need, Frances Miranda Gon—er, what are we even supposed to call you?" In an emergency, it seemed particularly insane to go through nine syllables merely to address the woman.

Frances Miranda Gonzagaga stared dreamily up at the ceiling.

"When I was a child longing for a friend," she whispered, "I always thought, 'I'll tell her to call me Mira.' Because that means 'Look!' in Spanish, and I always thought a friend would really see me." Slowly, slowly, slowly, she turned her head farther, to gaze directly at Josie. "Nobody has ever called me Mira."

"But you had whatnots," Max burst out. "You *invented* them! You could have told them to call you anything you wanted."

"Pah, whatnots," Frances Miranda Gonzagaga—er, no, *Mira*—said. She seemed to be trying to wave her hand dismissively, but she did it so weakly, her hand barely fluttered above the white sheet. "Whatnots were never my friends.

Or, they were more like . . . mirror friends. You know how a lonely child will sit in front of a mirror and make faces and hold out her hands and babble, and pretend that the image in the mirror is a friend responding?"

Josie, Ivy, Lucinda, and Lola nodded; Max and Ashley looked surprised.

"Do you know how old I was when I fashioned my first whatnot?" Mira asked. "I was twelve. And for years after that, I thought, 'I just need to come up with a better design, I just need to improve my skill with robotics, I just need stronger AI. . . .' But, alas, it was my starting premise that was flawed. I didn't need better whatnots. I needed . . . humans. And by then . . ."

Mira's ancient lips puckered. Josie wasn't sure the old woman could form a single other word. But she did.

"By then," Mira repeated, her voice lowering into a barely audible whisper, "by then it was too late."

"It's not too late," Josie said, though truthfully she wasn't sure. The bossy whatnot's words, "None of us are getting any younger here," made more sense now. That whatnot had been talking about Frances Miranda Gonzagaga, not Josie or her friends.

But surely, if Mira could manage that burst of words, she wasn't that desperately sick, was she?

She could still be rescued, couldn't she?

Ivy and Lucinda must have been thinking along the same lines, because they sprang toward the hospital bed. Lucinda took Mira's papery thin wrist in her own hands and quickly reported, "Her pulse is weak, but it's steady." Ivy felt Mira's forehead and added, "Her fever's not *that* high."

"Wow," Ashley said. "You can tell that without a thermometer or fancy blood-pressure machine or—"

"Our dad's a nurse," Lucinda said, the pride clear in her voice. "A nurse's aide, anyway. He taught us all sorts of things. He says sometimes the human touch is better because the machines can go hinky. . . ."

"Huh," Ashley said. "I don't think my parents have ever taught me *anything* useful like that. They say machines are better than humans at everything. Which . . . could be why they tried to hire whatnots."

"I think Mira needs real nurses," Ivy said, as if offering a professional opinion. "Real nurses, real doctors . . ."

"You have doctors and nurses helping you already, right?" Max asked anxiously. "All sorts of medical people who come in just for you . . ."

"I have . . . the whatnots," Mira said haltingly. "They *try*. But you know, I never anticipated them needing any more than a fifth-grade education, and . . . then when they did, I was too sick to give them upgrades. They ran my business, they took care of me, they took care of *you*. . . ." Now she was looking only at Josie, Ivy, and Lucinda.

"So what Josie won was . . . the chance to take care of you?" Ashley asked. She grimaced as if she could barely hold herself back from rolling her eyes.

"Yes, yes, we should talk about winning before it's too late," Mira said. But her voice trailed off. She blinked, and for a moment it seemed like she might not open her eyes again.

But then she did. She just seemed lost afterward, peering around in a baffled way.

"Josie answered your question," Lola reminded her. "Josie *understood*. Just like you expected. You said she was 'the one,' way back when Josie was about to have her first day of kindergarten. I'm sure it was you who wrote that. I analyzed the digital underpinnings of that text."

"You knew how to do that with only a fifth-grade education?" Max asked.

Lola gazed humbly down at the ground.

"I might have . . . enhanced myself a little," she admitted. "Because I thought it would help Josie."

"Is there a phone here now?" Josie asked, gazing around. "Can we call an ambulance?"

"No, no, no phone," Mira murmured. "Oh, my, this is awkward. . . ." Painstakingly, she lifted her head from the pillow and gazed directly at one child after another. "Josie, I did write that you could be 'the one' the night before you started kindergarten, the same time I asked that you be seated beside Max. But I wrote that about Ivy, too, the first time I saw her draw a castle. And I wrote it about Lucinda when I saw her displaying leadership skills as far back as preschool."

"So you just meant . . . I could be the one who'd become Max's friend," Josie said. The words felt heavy in her mouth. "And you thought Ivy could be his friend, too. And Lucinda could be Ashley's friend."

This was strange—she *was* Max's friend. She was glad they were friends. But it made her feel like a fake whatnot again, to think that being his friend was the only way she mattered.

Or that Ivy and Lucinda didn't matter outside their friendships with Max or Ashley either.

That, as poor kids, they had to have rich friends to be important.

This *was* as bad as being a fake whatnot.

"No, no, no," Mira moaned, as if she were in physical pain now. "I wanted you all to be friends, of course, but . . . that isn't why I wrote 'she could be the one' about any of you. I also wrote that about Ashley when I saw her make friendship bracelets for everyone in her class. And I wrote 'He could be the one' about Max when I saw how happy he was just playing in a mud puddle. I . . . ended up writing it at one time or another about every child. Every child in every school run by the Whatnot Corporation—every school that was actually just full of real, human kids."

"Then what did it even mean?" Lola asked.

"The one who . . ." Mira seemed so weak again. She seemed incapable of saying anything else.

Or maybe she was just overcome with shyness?

Suddenly, Josie understood.

"You mean, the one who could be *your* friend," Josie blurted out. "You were still looking for a *human* friend!"

"You're an adult, and you still wanted a friendship bracelet?" Ashley asked doubtfully. "You still wanted to play in mud puddles?"

Mira had tears in her eyes.

"I never fit in anywhere as a child," she said. "I never even tried. I never looked for anyone else who loved gears and gadgets and, and the whole idea of androids as much as I did. I was too shy. Too afraid of being rejected. I always locked myself away with my androids and hid behind them. Then, even though the whatnots I invented disappointed me, I thought they still could be like 'starter friends' for other kids—like the training wheels on bicycles. I wanted everyone in the world to have the friends I lacked! But the whatnots didn't help anyone else, either. Kids . . . need . . . kids. They need to learn from one another. They need to make mistakes and be forgiven and do better the next time. But the Whatnot Corporation was already huge; my whatnot schools were already everywhere.

The parents I talked to wanted more and more whatnots. So I began . . . cheating. I brought in real kids to fake being whatnots—I told myself they were getting opportunities they wouldn't have otherwise. An *education* they wouldn't have otherwise. But I always knew . . . it wasn't fair."

"No, it wasn't," Lucinda said. But even she sounded more sad than angry now.

"But I would watch the kids in my schools, and I would think, 'Oh, what a good friend this child would make! What a good friend that child would make!'" Mira said. "I *wanted* to be friends with all of you! But . . . friendship is a two-way street. Who was I to want to be friends with any of you? When my corporation was lying to your parents? When my schools were forcing you to keep secrets from your best friends?"

Nobody said anything.

Then Lola ventured, "Maybe if . . ."

Mira waved her words away.

"No, let me finish," she said. "While I still can. All I had to offer, as a friend, was my whatnots and the Whatnot Corporation. I set up a . . . testing ground. I thought, if any child could make it through my maze and answer the final question, to know what I'd wanted from the very beginning, that child would win my friendship. And that child would win . . ."

"You're giving Josie the Whatnot Corporation?" Max

interrupted, his voice cracking with excitement.

"Yes," Mira said. "I am old, and I am about to die, and when I do, Josie will inherit everything I own. Lola, would you—?" She gestured weakly to the side, pointing down. Was there something on the flat metal surface beneath the mattress?

Lola seemed to understand. She reached down and pulled out a sheaf of papers and a heavy, old-fashioned pen. She handed them to Mira.

"This makes everything official," Mira murmured, grasping the pen. She shuffled to the last page of the stack of papers and painstakingly began writing: *F r a n c . . .*

Josie watched the letters flow so slowly out of Mira's pen.

Now I can help my dad the way I've always wanted, she thought. *Now I won't have to worry about taking any more tests to get into a good middle school. And I can share with Ivy and Lucinda, too. . . .*

Frances Miranda Gonzagaga had so many letters in her name. Josie had time to remember changing Max's name tag, all those years ago in kindergarten when she told him it'd be easier to go by "Max" than "Maximilian." She had time to remember all her nights of huddling alone in her hidden room beneath the "charging station" drawer, while her father tried to sound cheerful at the other end of a phone line. She had time to remember saying to Ivy, "You're just a whatnot," and having Ivy say back to her, "You're just a whatnot, too."

Josie had time to remember all that, and Frances Miranda Gonzagaga was just now starting on the *G* of Gonzagaga.

And there was still time.

Josie jumped up and dived toward the hospital bed. She yanked the stack of papers from under Mira's pen, which turned the beginnings of the *G* into a long, thick, dark line running down the page. While everyone else stared at her in astonishment, Josie lifted the papers high in the air and ripped them exactly in half.

"No!" Josie screamed. "I don't want the Whatnot Corporation! You can't give it to me!"

SIXTY-TWO

Max the Friend (and Josie, Still Being a Friend, Too)

"Josie, have you gone nuts?" Max asked. "You're giving up the chance to be rich!"

He wanted to add, "Yeah, the Whatnot Corporation has problems, but you'd be in charge! You could fix everything!"

But before he could say anything else, the room exploded.

Not *literally*. It was just that confetti burst from the walls, and colorful streamers and balloons dropped from the ceiling. Trumpets and trombones shot out from the doorframe, blasting out bursts of triumphant music.

Everyone froze in place, confetti and streamers in their hair and on their clothes, balloons gently bonking against their heads.

And then Lola began to laugh.

"Oh, I see!" she chortled. "*This* was the real final test. Friendship isn't something you can buy or bribe your way into. Josie becoming Mira's friend—it wouldn't be *because* Mira gave Josie the Whatnot Corporation. True friends become friends because they genuinely like each other. And now Josie has passed this test, so . . ."

"So I really will give her everything I have," Mira finished, beaming at everyone. Even she had confetti stuck in her white hair. "Josie, you have restored my faith in humanity. And . . ." She chuckled. "You should have known that I of all people would make this transfer electronically."

She gestured again to Lola, and Lola rolled over close to the bed again. She turned around, and pulled her shawl and hair to the side. Mira reached up and touched some sort of release, and a screen and tiny keyboard unfolded from the back of Lola's neck. It was as if Lola had had a miniature laptop embedded in her body, which could spring out like some hidden tool on a Swiss army knife.

"You were linked into the internet this entire time?" Ashley gasped to Lola.

"I . . . wasn't allowed to tell," Lola said ruefully.

Josie ignored them both, and raced to Mira's side.

And then Josie clasped Mira's hand, gently pulling it away from the screen and keyboard.

"I wasn't just trying to give the right answer for a test," Josie said. She sat down on the hospital bed, still holding Mira's hand. "I really meant what I said. I don't want the Whatnot Corporation."

"What?" Mira said. Her smile drooped. Her eyes swam

with confusion. And pain. "But . . . but . . . would it really be that hard to be my friend?"

"That has nothing to do with this," Josie said, gesturing at the screen. "I'm eleven years old. I don't know anything about running a corporation!"

"You've got a fifth-grade education, and that's all any of us whatnots have, and we've been running it for years," Lola protested. "Even though . . . maybe . . . we didn't run it all that well. . . ."

"Josie, my dad would help you," Max volunteered.

"My parents probably would, too," Ashley agreed. "They're in technology—they would have all sorts of ideas for you."

Josie turned to look toward Lucinda and Ivy. Lucinda gulped.

"Josie, if you're going to say that thing about how, really, we all deserve to win, you don't have to," Lucinda said. "*I* wouldn't have passed that last test."

"But . . . the way the Whatnot Corporation made its money . . . ," Josie whimpered. "All those poor, lonely children like Lucinda and Ivy and me. All the parents like ours who gave up years with their kids, just for the hope that we could have better lives as adults. All those moments of our growing-up time that our families can never get back . . ."

Max squirmed. He had never known anyone was being hurt to help him. His *parents* had never known. But Frances

Miranda Gonzagaga had known, and she . . .

Is really, really sorry, he thought.

"You could give all the money away," Mira murmured to Josie. Once again, she had tears in her eyes. "You could make up for my mistakes."

Josie shook her head, as stubborn as Max had ever seen her.

"No," she said, even more firmly this time.

"You don't think it's enough to pay people back?" Ivy asked, her eyes intent on Josie's.

Max felt a familiar tiny stab of jealousy, because Josie and Ivy were just looking at each other for answers. Not him.

But that was fair, because Ivy and Josie had had shared experiences Max couldn't understand.

Not yet, anyway. But he was going to try.

Max walked over to Mira's bed. He patted Mira's right hand, the one Josie wasn't clutching.

"I don't want to have anything to do with the Whatnot Corporation," he said. "But Mira, I'll be your friend. And, Josie—"

He peered in her direction, still seeing the girl who'd rushed to his side in kindergarten. The girl who'd been at his side for the past six years. His best friend.

Who was also a totally independent person who would make up her own mind about what she thought about everything.

Always.

"And, Josie, you know I'll always be your friend, no matter what," he said.

"Good," Josie said. "But I really wasn't worried about *that* anymore."

"And I know you'll do whatever's right," Max finished.

Mira sighed, and snuggled down into her blankets like a woman planning to disappear.

"Then it's settled," she whispered. "Josie will take over the Whatnot Corporation and fix all my mistakes. Thank you. Thank you . . . my friend. *All* my friends."

She closed her eyes.

But then Josie jerked on the old woman's arm. Mira's eyes flew back open.

"I said *no!*" Josie repeated. "I am not going to take over the Whatnot Corporation and fix all your mistakes. Because . . . you're not going to die! You're going to live, and fix all your mistakes yourself! And you're going to be friends with all of us for years to come!"

SIXTY-THREE

The Narrator's Aside

Josie was right. The end.

SIXTY-FOUR

The Narrator's Aside

What's that? You're still here?

And you want *more*?

Good grief. Is a narrator's work never done?

Okay, okay, I'll admit, there is a bit more to the story.

All the kids—and I—finally convinced Mira that she should get checked out by real professional medical personnel before giving up on life. It turns out, it probably is not a good idea for anyone to drop out of school before sixth grade. Or for anybody who's sick to rely on medical opinions from people—er, androids—who don't know what they're talking about. Max ran to get Nurse Beverly, who was soon freed along with Max's parents. And Nurse Beverly quickly and expertly diagnosed a huge part of Mira's problem as . . . dehydration.

Water—it's good for you!

That wasn't the only issue, but every problem Mira had was treatable.

She had absolutely nothing fatally wrong with her.

Mira ended up keeping control of the Whatnot Corporation—or maybe I should say, taking back control from all of the Model 82958s. She never reactivated them, and she certainly never reactivated the bully models.

But she didn't close any of her schools.

Instead, with help from both Max's parents and Ashley's, she negotiated deals with every single set of rich parents who thought they'd been paying to keep whatnot androids around their children.

Again and again, she told them, "If you don't tell anyone about the Whatnot Corporation, I won't tell anyone you didn't trust your child around real children. And, hey, let's all work together to keep all the kids in the schools they already love, with all the friends they've cared about all along."

For the first time, she got patents on all her brilliant work, and turned around and shared her expertise with others. That launched a million articles about "The Mystery Genius of AI," and lots of speculation about who she really was and how she'd come out of nowhere to upend the technology world. But Mira had no desire to go around talking about herself, so she just let the technology world wonder.

She was much more concerned with making things right with Josie and her dad, Ivy and Lucinda's family, and the families of all the other kids who had ever pretended to be whatnots. Mira decided to divide up all the money she'd earned from running whatnot schools over the years, and she gave every family their share. It went to so many people that no one ended up getting a fortune. Josie and Ivy and Lucinda did not get to live in houses as big as Max's and Ashley's. They didn't get to fly around in private, pilotless helicopters of their own.

But they got enough to be comfortable. They got enough that they didn't have to think about money all the time, before and after every decision they made.

And maybe you're also wondering, what about . . . me?

Mira fixed the broken parts of my face as soon as she had recovered enough to do so. (*She* understood why I wouldn't want to be reminded of bullies every time I looked in a mirror, even though the Model 82958s thought it didn't matter when I was only working behind the scenes.) And then I moved in with Josie and her dad. I wasn't there to take care of Josie—or rather, not exclusively. We made a pact to take care of *each other*. She says it's like she finally has the big sister she always wanted. But she will grow and change, and I won't. Josie says that's fine—she always wanted a little sister, too.

But Mira was baffled that I didn't shut off with all the other whatnots. She swore she'd programmed each and every one of us the same way, to shut down when some child made it through the maze and answered the Model 82958s' question correctly. I *should* have stopped working the moment Josie said the word "friend," and the door to Mira's hospital room clicked open.

But I didn't. Evidently some of my own reprogramming prevented that.

It was Ivy and Lucinda's little brother, Casper, who had the best theory about what happened.

We were all having a picnic together—Mira, Josie and her dad, Max and his parents, Ashley and her parents, Ivy's entire family, and of course, me—while everyone tried to figure out why I hadn't stopped.

"It's like you were too real for that," Josie argued.

"Wreal?" Ivy's brother repeated. He toddled over to his diaper bag, and came back with a battered book, a copy of *The Velveteen Rabbit* that had belonged to his grandfather and his mother and Ivy and Lucinda before him. "Like Wabbit! Wuv makes you Wreal!"

"Or . . . friendship!" Max and Josie said, speaking so completely in unison that everyone else laughed.

"Is it because I'm friends with all of you, or because you're all friends with me?" I asked, trying to keep my voice from trembling.

"We all fwends togevver!" Casper announced.

And everyone agreed he'd figured out the answer.

It bothers Mira that she cannot quantify this scientifically, that she cannot prove it one way or another. But that doesn't mean she doubts it.

Some truths can only be felt.

Even by an android.

EPILOGUE

Josie and Max and Their Family and Friends

It was the last day of summer vacation, and Max was having a party at his pool.

To the casual observer, it probably looked about the same as the party he'd had on the last day of fifth grade: same pool, same sunshine, same kids. Same shrieks of laughter at bellyflops and same cheers for elegantly executed dives.

But everything was different.

Nobody was keeping secrets.

Nobody was wondering what food they'd have on their family dinner tables when they went home that night.

Nobody was worrying about what school they'd land in next, or fearing that they might disappoint their family.

Everyone was just . . .

Happy.

At the end of the party, Max lay on his stomach across the middle of a swimming-pool raft, his arms and legs dangling into the water. Josie leaped out of the water and flopped across the raft beside him.

"The grown-ups are arriving," she announced, watching parents stream in through the opulent gates and summon one kid after another from the pool. Ivy was still nearby, turning the dots of water splashed onto the concrete into an artistic design. But Jack, who'd also become a good friend over the course of the summer, was already out of the pool and toweling off. Other kids were waving and shouting their goodbyes.

"Enh, your dad'll go on talking to Mira forever, so *we've* still got time," Max said, tilting his head to indicate the row of beach chairs where Josie's dad and Mira were huddled together under an umbrella. Both of them alternated between peering proudly out at all the kids in the pool, and nodding excitedly at one another. Mira claimed Josie's dad was the first person she'd ever met who loved building things as much as she did. When the two of them got together, it was like they had their own language that nobody else could understand.

"No, look—you can tell Mira's getting tired," Josie said, watching the old lady carefully. "My dad protects her as much as he does me, now." She rolled her eyes. "I give him two minutes before he yells, 'Josie, time to go!'"

"That's okay," Max said, as if he needed to remind himself. "You can tell him your family lives so close by now, surely you can stay a *little* longer."

Once Josie and her dad had gotten their share of the Whatnot Corporation money, Josie's dad had bought the house that Max had thought Josie lived in all along—the one beside the school. Max and Josie both thought that was funny. And . . . great. Over the summer Josie's dad had turned the house into an apartment building for lots of families of former fake whatnots, including Ivy and Lucinda's.

"And," Josie told Max with a reassuring shrug, "we'll see each other tomorrow at school."

All the parents of the kids from Max and Josie's fifth-grade class had agreed to just expand the school through sixth grade and keep everyone together. The adults used words like "transition year" and "while everyone adjusts." Max sometimes felt a few butterflies in his stomach thinking about what changes he might face in *seventh* grade. But Josie wasn't worried.

And it made thinking about the start of sixth grade really, really easy.

Max ran his hand back and forth in the water, creating tiny ripples that barely rocked their raft.

"We really will be friends forever now, right?" he asked.

"If it's anything *I* can control," Josie said.

At the beginning of the summer, that would have been more than enough of an answer for Max. Because he knew he would always want that, too.

But there's something about the last day of summer that makes everything seem uncertain. It makes you feel like anything could end. And Max had learned so much that summer about himself and Josie and the rest of the world; he saw all sorts of ripples now below the surface of his peaceful life that had always been invisible to him before.

"Josie, it really wasn't fair to you, how everything turned out," he burst out. "Back in that maze, and with the test in Mira's hospital room—you *won*! And you didn't end up getting anything more than anyone else!"

"Do you think I care about that?" Josie asked. She watched her dad and Mira together, his thick head of dark hair bent close to her wispy white curls, his young but weathered face and her old, wrinkled one carrying matching lively expressions. She saw Max's mom bend down to admire Ivy's artwork; she saw Nurse Beverly and Lola greeting Ivy's dad. "Don't you know I wanted everyone to be happy?"

"But you could have been in charge," Max said. "You could have told all the whatnots what to do. And all the rich parents who wanted to keep things secret." He looked around at the kids in the pool, the ones halfway in and halfway out, and the ones walking away arm in arm with their parents. "But this way, we're all still stuck as kids. We'll have to wait until we're grown-ups to decide things for ourselves. To make our own world however we want it to be."

"What are you talking about?" Josie laughed. In the slant of sunlight coming from lower and lower in the sky, everything around them felt quicksilver and changeable. In a moment, she might decide to upend the raft and send both her and Max tumbling into the water. Or she might lean her head against his shoulder, and keep rocking peacefully in the waves. It was, indeed, her choice. Just as it'd been her choice to tell Max she wasn't a whatnot. Just as it'd been her choice to sneak over to the school with Ivy.

And just as it'd been her choice to rescue Mira, and set in motion everything that led to Josie being able to stay friends with Max. And to get Mira to fix the Whatnot Corporation. And to become friends with Ivy, Mira, Lola, Lucinda, Ashley, Jack, Max's parents, Ivy's parents . . .

The list went on and on.

She turned to Max, and somehow in that split second, she could see him as the kindergartener he'd once been, as well as the teenager he was about to become. And the kid he was in this very moment.

Her friend.

And he could see her as she really was, too.

"Max, can't you tell?" she asked. "We're making our own world *now*."

ACKNOWLEDGMENTS

I wrote *The School for Whatnots* at the end of 2019 and spent a good chunk of my 2020 pandemic lockdown time revising the book. So my first inclination, thinking about who I want to acknowledge here, is a little skewed: I am so grateful to Josie, Max, Ivy, and Lola for hanging out with me during that heavily restricted time!

Okay, I do actually realize that they are only fictional. And there are several real people I am grateful to as well. I appreciate both my agent, Tracey Adams, and editor, Katherine Tegen, for their thoughtful insights and suggestions about the book. I was also grateful to receive comments and advice from Candice Roma, a sensitivity reader with Salt & Sage Books.

Additionally, I'd like to thank everyone in various departments at HarperCollins who worked on the book, including Sara Schonfeld, Kathryn Silsand, Mark Rifkin, Christina MacDonald, David Curtis, Amy Ryan, Vanessa Nuttry, Susan Bishansky, Kathy Campbell, Aubrey Churchward, and Emily Mannon. And I love the cover illustration from Rebecca Mock.

Also, as always, I'm grateful to my family and friends for their support all along the way. Many of them I was connecting with only virtually during the pandemic, but seeing their faces never failed to cheer me. I'm especially grateful to my two local writers groups, who temporarily turned into online writers groups: Jody Casella, Julia DeVillers, Linda Gerber, Lisa Klein, Erin McCahan, Jenny Patton, Edith Pattou, Nancy Roe Pimm, Natalie D. Richards, and Linda Stanek.

And thank YOU for reading this book! I hope you consider Josie, Max, Ivy, and Lola your friends now, too!

Read more Margaret Peterson Haddix in her thrilling
MYSTERIES OF TRASH AND TREASURE series!

The Beginning

If Colin hadn't found the first shoebox, nothing important would have happened that summer.

He and Nevaeh never would have met.

They never would have found the *other* shoebox.

They never would have made a secret pact behind their parents' backs.

They never would have solved a single mystery.

They never would have . . . well, it doesn't matter what else wouldn't have happened, does it? Nothing else would have happened.

But Colin did find the shoebox, hidden under the floorboard in a stranger's attic.

And that changed everything.

Colin's Summer, Day One

"Colin! Up and at 'em!"

Colin only bothered to open one eye, and that only to half-mast. His mother hovered over him, her grin much too wide and excited for six a.m.

It was the first day of summer. The. Very. First. Day.

"Mo-om," Colin moaned. Even that took more energy than he wanted to use. "Seriously. I'm old enough to stay home by myself this year."

"If you're old enough for that," she countered, "you're old enough to work."

Mom was already snapping his blinds open. Now she was in his closet, pulling a shirt off a hanger. Now she snatched a pair of shorts from his dresser drawer. Now she had his whole outfit for the day arrayed on his chair. Colin would have actually had to roll over to see, but he was pretty sure she'd also fished his sneakers out from under the bed and lined them up beneath the chair, perfectly parallel and perfectly aimed for the door.

And she'd done all that before he'd had a chance to blink.

That's how Mom was: a tiny dynamo. She *always* moved as fast as a hummingbird. Her favorite words were "lickety-split" and "pronto." (Recently she'd been studying French by podcast and begun saying "Vite!" a lot, too.)

Colin's favorite words were "wait" and "Let me think about that for a minute. . . ."

Colin still didn't move.

"Colin, remember . . . ," Mom said.

That was all it took. Because Colin did remember. He remembered how Mom had kept her head bowed, not even looking him in the eye the night she'd told him they couldn't afford the day camp program he'd gone to the past several summers. He remembered how many times he'd heard her take a call from a client and say in her bright, cheery Professional Voice, "Let me step into another room, to protect your privacy. . . ." And then not gotten far enough away before saying in a smaller, deflated tone that Colin could still overhear, "So you won't be needing my services, after all?"

He remembered that times were hard and small businesses were in trouble and that this summer Mom just couldn't hire all the workers it would take to stay afloat.

He remembered—though she hadn't quite said it in so many words—that she needed his help.

Colin forced himself to sit up. He tried to stretch his mouth into an imitation of Mom's wide smile.

"I am so ready to move boxes!" he cried. "And clean houses! And do whatever else you want me to do! I live to work!"

Mom . . . giggled.

"Okay, laying it on a little thick there," she said, ruffling his thick, dark, curly hair that was almost exactly like hers, only shorter. "But you get an A for effort. I *knew* it'd be fun having more time together this summer."

Colin did not say, *Yeah, that's every twelve-year-old kid's fantasy, to spend more time working for his mom.*

He was too busy staring in horror at the red shirt she'd picked out for him to wear.

"A collar?" he asked. "You want me to move boxes in ninety-degree heat *wearing a shirt with a collar?*"

Mom smoothed a wrinkle Colin hadn't noticed in the shirt.

"Image, remember?" she said. "Ninety-nine percent of the reason someone would hire me instead of you-know-who is my company's image. Nobody would believe a four-foot-eleven female is going to be best at moving boxes, if that's all it's about."

Mom drew herself up to her full height—which Colin was pretty sure was only four foot ten and a half, but he wasn't going to argue. He'd been taller than her since he was nine.

He couldn't even remember how old he'd been the first time someone had said, "Wow. Looks like your little boy got his height from his dad," and his mom said, "Yep," in a way that made it clear there would be no follow-up questions.

Mom didn't talk about Dad.

Neither did Colin.

He'd learned not to talk too much about Mom's business, either. Way back in second grade, he'd given a speech in front of the whole class about her. He'd been so proud. He'd practiced again and again just saying the name of her company: Possession Curation. (In second grade, he'd still had a little trouble saying *s*'s properly.) He'd memorized her company motto—"You Deserve Only the Best"—and explained how helping people get rid of things that were old and broken and useless made it so their houses were cleaner, and they had more room, and they could enjoy having nice things instead.

And then the meanest kid in the class, a boy named Hunter, spoke up without even raising his hand. "He means his mom is a garbageman! Colin's mom picks up trash! She's a *woman* garbageman!"

While the other kids laughed, the teacher tried to explain that, first of all, the actual term was "garbage collector," and secondly, "There's nothing wrong with being a garbageman—er, collector—and certainly not anything wrong with a woman doing that. And, anyhow, that wasn't exactly what Colin was saying, was it, Colin?"

Hunter had called Colin "Garbage Boy" the rest of the school year, anyhow. But that wasn't even what hurt.

No, what hurt was when the nicest kid in the class, a girl named Shivani, raised her hand right after that. Colin could see by the earnest look on her face that she wanted to help. Her voice was so kind when she said, "Do you mean your mom is like that guy on TV? The Junk King?"

Colin had started shaking, and he'd actually shouted back at Shivani, "No! My mom is not like the Junk King! She's nothing like him at all!"

And then he'd run and hidden in the bathroom. Because how could he have shouted at someone like Shivani?

And how could anyone think Mom was like the Junk King?

"Earth to Colin," Mom said now. "Where'd you go, just then?"

"Just thinking," Colin said.

"Think and move at the same time," Mom said. She handed him his shirt and shorts. "Breakfast's in five minutes. I want to be out the door in twenty. We've got a lot to do today!"

Colin was not good at thinking and moving at the same time.

He wasn't particularly good at doing anything. He was best at just . . . being.

This was going to be the worst summer of his life.

2

Nevaeh's Summer, Day One

Nevaeh tucked the cereal box under her arm, plucked a spoon from the silverware drawer, and, without looking, reached into the cupboard for a bowl. Her hand met empty air and then, a bare shelf. She glanced toward the sink and yanked open the door of the dishwasher. More emptiness.

"Dad!" she hollered. "Did you sell our dishes again?"

"Found a better set," he called back from his narrow office at the other end of the hall. "Look in the boxes on the dining room table. Not the ones with the sticky note about sending them out for eBay, but—"

"Never mind," Nevaeh said. "I'll have toast."

"Roddy's using the toaster for his latest experiment, remember?" Nevaeh's older sister, Prilla, said behind her, where she was leaning into the refrigerator. "Something about trying to make it solar powered . . ."

"Bread, then!" Nevaeh said. "I'll have dry, boring, tasteless bread. . . ."

"Oh, no—not today, little sister," Prilla said, emerging from the refrigerator with an open jumbo-sized container of yogurt with exactly one serving left. She eased the cereal box away from Nevaeh, shook granola onto the yogurt, and spun back toward the fridge, muttering, "Let's see, the perfect topper . . . yes!" A moment later, she presented Nevaeh with the plastic yogurt container as if it were a crystal goblet. Prilla bowed, truly hamming it up. "A yogurt parfait, complete with whipped cream and a maraschino cherry on top. Fit for the youngest Junk Princess on her big day!"

Yeah, fit for a Junk Princess because it's in a plastic container, and I'm going to eat it with a spoon that Dad literally found at a junkyard, Nevaeh thought.

But how could she complain, when Prilla was being so nice?

"Thanks," Nevaeh muttered, taking a big bite that was mostly whipped cream.

"And while you eat," Prilla said, steering Nevaeh toward a chair at the kitchen table, "I'll French-braid your hair so it's out of your way. Unless you want to pull a Roddy."

"Not my style," Nevaeh said.

Roddy, who was Prilla's twin, shaved his head at the start of every summer. Their other two brothers, Axel and Dalton, went the man-bun route.

All the Greeveys (except Roddy, now) had the same thick, dark blond hair. Also: the same too-wide mouths; the same too-big noses; the same pale, prone-to-freckling skin; and the same constantly surprised-looking brown eyes. The first day of kindergarten, Nevaeh's teacher had done a double take, gasped, and then said, "There's no way you could pretend not to be a Greevey, is there?"

Nevaeh didn't want to pretend she wasn't a Greevey. She wasn't ashamed that Dad was the Junk King of Groveview, Ohio. She could easily ignore it when stupid kids at school made fun of the slogan he always used in his TV commercials: "Got junk you don't want anymore? I'll take it. I LOOOVE junk!"

She just didn't want to have anything to do with junk herself.

Usually Nevaeh liked it when Prilla braided her hair, but not today. Today, it felt like Prilla was pulling every strand too tightly.

Still, Nevaeh didn't let herself squirm away.

"You know this is a big deal for Dad, having all five of us work for him this summer," Prilla said. "You know he loves that little ceremony he made up with the scepter and all—'You are twelve now, old enough to join the family business, old enough to claim your royal title. . . .'"

"I *know*," Nevaeh said, a little too sharply.

She hadn't even been born yet the summer Axel turned twelve, but Dad liked reminding her that she'd been there for his ceremony, at least as a fetus. She'd been three when Dalton turned twelve, and seven when it was Prilla's and Roddy's turn. She could remember jumping up and down and cheering for the twins as if they really had inherited a throne.

Of course, back then she'd also half believed that the scepter Dad had welded together out of spare car parts truly was precious gold, and the "jewels" at the top were real diamonds and rubies, not see-through little toy balls from a gumball machine.

"Mom's home," Prilla said, glancing out the kitchen window at the car speeding in a cloud of dust down their gravel driveway. Prilla finished the braid and expertly wrapped a rubber band around the end. "You ready for this?"

No, Nevaeh thought.

"Sure," she said.

Everyone else came crowding into the kitchen: Mom, back early from her overnight shift as an X-ray tech at the hospital. Axel and his fiancée. Dalton and his current girlfriend, who probably wouldn't remain his girlfriend but would likely be invited to holiday dinners at the Greeveys' for the rest of her life, because that was how the Greeveys rolled. Roddy with his newly shaved head, which gleamed almost as much as the toaster he was carrying.

And then Dad swept down the hallway. He carried both the scepter made out of car parts and a shimmery crown made out of . . . were those old compact discs?

"Hear ye, hear ye," Dad announced. "On this joyous day, Nevaeh Lenore Greevey comes into her inheritance. Nevaeh Lenore, do you accept all the rights and responsibilities of being a Junk Princess?"

Never, Nevaeh thought.

But she looked around at all the people who looked like her. Tucked among them, Axel's fiancée and Dalton's girlfriend both looked like they wanted to laugh, but in a kind way.

This was Nevaeh's true inheritance: all these people loving her.

This was what it meant to be the Junk Princess.

"I do," Nevaeh said.

Dad placed the compact-disc crown on her head, and it fit as if it'd been waiting for her her entire life.

This is going to be the worst summer of my life, Nevaeh thought.

No. It was worse than that.

This was the start of every summer for the rest of her life being awful.

BOOKS BY BESTSELLING AUTHOR
MARGARET PETERSON HADDIX

MYSTERIES OF TRASH AND TREASURE SERIES

RUNNING OUT OF TIME SERIES

GREYSTONE SECRETS SERIES

KATHERINE TEGEN BOOKS
An Imprint of HarperCollins Publishers

harpercollinschildrens.com